T0082859

TRIBES OF MERMAIDS

Mark and Raquel Wehinger

authorHOUSE®

AuthorHouse™
1663 Liberty Drive
Bloomington, IN 47403
www.authorhouse.com
Phone: 833-262-8899

© 2021 Mark and Raquel Wehinger. All rights reserved.

No part of this book may be reproduced, stored in a retrieval system, or
transmitted by any means without the written permission of the author.

This is a work of fiction. All of the characters, names, incidents,
organizations, and dialogue in this novel are either the products
of the author's imagination or are used fictitiously.

Published by AuthorHouse 01/11/2022

ISBN: 978-1-6655-4807-6 (sc)
ISBN: 978-1-6655-4812-0 (e)

Library of Congress Control Number: 2021925830

Print information available on the last page.

Any people depicted in stock imagery provided by Getty Images are models,
and such images are being used for illustrative purposes only.
Certain stock imagery © Getty Images.

This book is printed on acid-free paper.

Because of the dynamic nature of the Internet, any web addresses or
links contained in this book may have changed since publication and
may no longer be valid. The views expressed in this work are solely those
of the author and do not necessarily reflect the views of the publisher,
and the publisher hereby disclaims any responsibility for them.

IN THE BEGINNING

Seventy percent of the earth is covered in water and eighty percent of the entire population on earth lives next to it or very close to the ocean or a body of water. Why do we need to live close to water to exist on this planet? The entire earth was once covered in water.

When a baby is born they hold their breath automatically when under the water, it is a behavior that is imprinted in our memories in the neuro transmitters in our brains. It could be in your DNA. Babies have the highest percentage of water of body mass at 78% water.

Why would sailors write logs, letters and tell stories about seeing and hearing a human looking female from the waist up and fish like bottom, signing coined Mermaids. Saving the lives of hundreds of sailors and killing untold others in the past fifteen thousand years. Are these stories true or are all the stories just a story to gain recommendation from others or many of these stories true and our government pacifically the U.S. Navy and Homeland Security investigations again hiding the truth about the existence of Mermaids because of their continued testing of Sonar around the world to see if they can destroy a possible enemies internal electrical and communications. So far they have succeeded in killing off whales up and down the Coast of California around the Hawaiian Islands, Washington State down to Mexico of which thousands of Dolphins and possibly Mermaids, Mermen around the world.

My name is Robert Walters, Ph.D. and my wife is Brandy Walters, Ph.D. we are research scientist with NOAA stationed on Oahu, Hawaii Islands. It is our agencys' goal to research earth systems in our climate, weather and oceans. Our daughter Jing is working on her doctorate degree at Hawaii Pacific University in Honolulu Oahu.

Brandy and I adopted Jing when she was only two years old in the Philippines. Her birth name is Raquel. It was Christmas time in the Philippines and Christmas songs were playing everywhere, Raquel would hear the song Jingle bells and would start singing the song nonstop so we gave her the nick name Jing for Jingle Bells and it stuck so everyone knows her as Jing. She is every guys dream girl, long black hair, gold skin, pearl white teeth smart and a world class surfer, placing in the North Shore Reef Hawaiian Pro, Winning The Roxy Pro North Shore and North Shore "Ko'Olau Loa."

We live in a small house on the North Shore of Oahu across the street from the ocean.

We drive NOAA Toyota's to and from work and bicycle to the store for anything. Jing drives an old Toyota pickup with three hundred thousand miles on it to and from school.

The Toyota also carries her surf boards to North Shore.

I was sitting on the lanai which is a porch with furniture as most of us locals live in our Lanai's. I was laying back in my favorite chair with some old pillow when Brandy came out to the lanai and said.

"Robert let's get some beer at the market, we are out. Do you want to bicycle there, she said with her smile that was so warm and loving that made one wanting to bicycle to the store.

"Sure, I need some exercise today it seems all I do anymore is read reports about how many whales have washed up on shores around the islands." Robert replies smiling back.

In the small communities around the island all the locals know each other, and surfers are really in tune with the weather. They know current trends in wave action and sharks in the area. All the local girls follow Jing where ever she is surfing which is usually daily.

"Hay Brandy what time is it because I want to watch that special about Mermaids on the history channel, it's about NOAA and our doctor Mathews and his assistance." He ask Brandy.

"It is 4pm Hawaii time, it is time to get the suds my stud." Brandy reaches over and kiss Robert suciding him into bicycling to the store.

"Ok I am going right now." Robert bicycles to the store, buys the beer and returns home to watch the history channel. Jing is home from school. She also works for NOAA on a research project for her Ph.D. dissertation.

Brandy asked Robert to buy her a Diet Pepsi.

While opening a couple beers Robert and Brandy sit down on the couch and Jing drinks her Diet Pepsi as all of them watch the program. Robert has taken the time to record it. As they watch and joke with each other they notice who the actors are and who replaced the actual persons who work for NOAA. They all laugh together but soon sit on the edge of the couch with serious faces looking at each other after the completion of the so called documentary. At this point in time neither Robert, Brandy or Jing have a clue what they are about to get involved in the research of Mermaids. After viewing the program Robert said to Brandy.

"Babe what do you think about that." Looking at Brandy with his eyes wide open and looking confused "Wow." "Jing what do you think." Brandy ask. "If that film is real I want to study and research this, I guess we call them Mermaids.

"Of course we call them Mermaids or all the little girls around the world will be disappointed and we would be bared from Disney Land for life Jing replays with a smile.

Both Robert and Brandy clap and smile at Jing for her comments.

"I can't believe half that stuff, like the kids cell phone pictures of the Mermaid on the beach and all of a sudden she raises up and growls, right I just don't know Mom, I would have to see it myself. Jing replies. "What do you think Brandy." Robert ask. "I agree with Brandy, I need proof that we either see in person or proof of evidence that can be recorded, measured and verified by us." Brandy replies.

"Spoken like a true researcher." Robert said.

"Where is Dr. Mathews, let's get him involved in this….." Brandy is interrupted by the telephone ring. Brandy answers the phone.

"Hello, yes this is Dr. Brandy Walters, she listens.

"Ok, ok, yes sir, thank you doctor, see you next week." Brandy hangs up and looks at Robert and Jing with a smile, picks up her beer and takes a drink.

"We are now assigned to the marine life division now

because of that documentary, that was our boss Dr. Wilson he said the White House called him and they want a study now about these Mermaids so let us get all the books we can on Mermaids and make a study of them. "The good doctor said to keep our study classified. Not to discuss the study with anyone." "You too Jing, The director said we get to use you as our research assistance.

"Make sure we do not discuss our study or mention the word Mermaids among our staff the doctor ordered. I am sure the Navy has put their own people into NOAA by now to see if we have any more evidence or are talking about their research that is obviously killing the whales all over the world when they test there Sonar into the ocean.

"What do you think Brandy!" Robert looks at Brandy for reassurances."

"Sure let us do it but you remember Robert to keep your mouth shut, you are always the one who ask the stupid questions or blurts out something and gives the whole story away." Brandy laughs at Robert.

Robert just shakes his head and looks out through the lanai to the ocean with a curious look on his face wondering if out there Mermaids are in the waves.

The next few weeks Robert, Brandy and Jing gather books from the NOAA library and the University of Hawaii Pacific University about Mermaids. The entire living room is covered in books stacked on two table and laying on the floor everywhere.

"Don't forget babe to question everything." Robert tells Jing.

"I will Dad, but don't we need to develop some type of hypothesis don't we." Jing ask.

"No we are going to follow Dr. Mathews research design and when we have scientific proof that such creatures exist in our oceans we will then develop some type of hypothesis. We can develop our research design or where do we start. In other words it is not so important that we can test our data at this point. Do these marine and lake siren or water spirits exist but how and why they are in the ocean and our lakes if that is our hypothesis or part of it." Robert concludes.

After writing notes a few minutes Brandy turns around in her chair and see's her sleepy dog "Ariel" come walking into the living room. Ariel is a half pug and half Boston Terrier rescue dog, with black and gray hair and always makes a funny noise when she is breathing hard. She totally loves Brandy and Jing. She just put's up with Robert. She walks over to Brandy's' chair and nudges Brandy on the leg asking her to pick her up. Brandy picks her up and continues writing while Robert smiles and said.

"Hay babe I thought that dog died or something it is only three pm, did she even eat today?" Robert smiles.

Jing looks at her dad and said.

"You are horrible dad, poor Ariel." Jing smiles at her dad.

"Of course, I feed her this morning and we went for a walk down to the beach, she even played in the surf with me, so there, you can keep that old fat cat of yours." Brandy tells Robert smiling back.

"Buy the way where is my fat cat, I haven't seen him and…." Robert is interrupted by Brandy.

"Remember that stake I feed you for breakfast, you eat him Robert." Brandy and Jing laughs out loud.

"Noooo", Robert yells out in play and says' "Get back to work or we will never figure it out." after several days of research by all of them between doing the NOAA scheduled research and their research at home they have not proven yet one way or the other that these amphibian creatures existed in our waters around the world. We know that seventy percent of the world is covered in water and at one time. The entire world was covered in water according to the over a hundred religions. Robert is sitting at a table out on the lanai with his cat named "Fat Cat" because he is a male has been neutered and eats all day and lays around the house, usually on Roberts books. Brandy walks into the lanai and said.

"So I see Fat Cat made it out here on the lanai babe." while she pets the cat.

"So do you have an opinion one way or another yet?" Robert ask.

"Not yet, I am still working on it. I will have or write one when you finish yours' ok."

Brandy tells Robert. "With all the research of written material about saving of sailors by the Mermaids, they act like life guards at the beach all ways on duty for all the sailors overboard. Brandy comments.

"Lets focus on all the rescues then work on one direction. "Right." then investigate efficacy of the researchers information, ok babe." Robert ask Brandy.

"Lets do that honey." Brandy replies with a smile.

"Alright for the sake of argument do we believe that Mermaids exists in the ocean?" Robert looks at Brandy with a serious look and Fat Cat looks up at Brandy waiting for her response also.

"After reading everything I have and even though some put this in the category of myths, legends and folk lore like the big foot legend. This data has been recorded for a thousands years in every ocean and major lakes all over the world at times when no one had talked with others in that country about such sightings. I believe Mermaids may exists Robert." Brandy said with authority.

"Ok I do too, so we will start with Dr. Mathews notes for our direction. With a statement that with over whelming documentation about sightings of these Mermaid creatures, and for the sake of argument we believe that Mermaids exists in our oceans and some lakes. Jing interrupt her dad and said.

"I believe they do exist however I have some reservations, even though Dr. Mathews has proof they exist It is not that I don't believe his findings, but I need to see the evidence myself." Jing concluded. Jing continues saying.

"Look Dad, all the material I have read dating back hundreds of years by hundreds of different folks in countries before world communications. For example the fishermen who killed a great white shark only to find home made spears in its body just like all the ones reported over the last thousand years in different incidents and accounts reported by the public who had no financial stake but to warn others going out into the ocean.

Fifteen thousand years ago in Egypt's mountainous in the plateau caves and inside those caves are picture drawn on the walls showing fights between humans with two legs and humans with fins fighting with bows and arrows spears being killed.

"I also believe Mermaids exists according to many other researchers and the Navy

Documentations." Robert looks and Jing then Brandy and said.

"What did you just say about documentation from Jing ".

"Yes, a friend of mine or should I say a fellow surfer told me that he actually saw what appeared to be a real Mermaids in a tank at a Navy installation on the east coast. So I asked him if he had any documentation to prove that they exist and he said he would prove it to me and he did with this." Jing hands Robert a file that said. Secret.

They all read the document and now realize that the Navy has been sitting on proof that Mermaids exist and they have a live Mermaids in a secret Navy base. Robert looks at Jing and Brandy and said.

"We must keep this document secret. No pun intended. We will copy it then return it to your friend Jing. We must never discuss the contents of this material. Jing you should tell your friend the same thing and encourage him to return the document to the Navy files ok."

Brandy looks at both of them and smiles and said

"Now that we know Mermaids exist, all we need to do is independently prove that Mermaids exist somewhere in the world, right" Jing ask.

Robert and Brandy look at each other nod their heads and smile.

"We will need to visually record the physical being and test the DNA of such so that other scientist can further investigate the species.

Ladies we need to figure out where we are going to search for these species. where they are likely to live in our oceans and lakes." Robert said.

Brandy ask Robert now sitting petting Fat Cat while Brandy and Jing's dog Ariel is nudging her leg again for her to pick her up on her lap. Jing picks up Ariel. Just then Brandy said.

"Let's take a walk down to the beach and think about where to start our investigation." Brandy suggests.

"I think that is a great idea, let me get us a couple of bottles of beer to take with us."

Robert responds.

Jing speaks up and tells her Dad.

"How about a Diet Pepsi, aspartame free for me."

"You got it my dear." Replies Robert

While sitting now on the beach looking out at the waves coming in with a few surfers in the water Brandy turns to Robert and ask.

"What is the number one issue or event that seems to yell out to you in each book we have researched, that one thing Robert that all the witness and sighting tells us."

Brandy ask Robert looking up at him with her big brown eyes and long blond hair like a surfer girl. Brandy puts her arm around Jing and ask the same question.

"The one thing that all people reported in every incident on every content in every language was that these Mermaids looked like females from the waist up and like fish from the waist down. Also they were shy and swam very fast." Jing reports.

"I read the same thing, but each incident involving Mermaids involved some type of event such as a man overboard, ship sinking, fire on the wooden ship and either reported the killing of a seamen or the saving of one" Brandy reports.

"Now what did you read Robert." Ask Brandy

"They seem to always be around ship wrecks." Robert is interrupted by Brandy.

"I mean how would you describe them. Their physical and behavioral things that have been reported like always being on ship wrecks not saving the sailors but drowning them not being beautiful but scary looking with sharp teeth and human like faces being half fish from the waist down with breathing holes developed with web hands and sharks being there only enemy. "Robert, I do subscribe to that theory we watched and when the earth was covered in water as described in the bible and religious writing all over the world support that data I believe some type of humans took to the oceans during this period to survive and seven million years ago they developed into a species of half human and half fish to survive in the oceans and lakes of the world., but you guys know what is driving me nuts is wondering where did the Navy get that Mermaid and what are they going to do with her." Brandy said.

Robert put up his hand as to stop for a minute, and said "Look you guys agreed not to discuss what we read ever and that means ever, I am sorry we need to honor that directive and our countries secrets. So please never to discuss it again. Think of it in these terms we have an edge on anyone trying to do this research in the entire world because we really know the truth. ok ladies." Robert said

Both ladies nod their heads and smile.

Jing nods her head, acknowledging Brandy further assessment of all the reporting of thousands of people all over the world seeing Mermaids in the ocean and lakes.

"Robert smiles and replies, "I read the same stuff Brandy and agree not explore other areas such as a possible missing link or such as we need to stick to research and then end our scientific investigation do you guys agree." Robert ask everyone.

"Yes, I do agree Robert. The French word for mother is mere suggesting the sea is our mother. These Mermaids have been treated as goddesses all over the world through the ages they are mentioned in art, music and even movies yet no one has a dead body or maybe our Navy has one." Brandy smiles at Jing and looks over at Robert.

"We are going to do everything we can to prove extensive one way or the other. Now I think we should send an email to all of our colleagues requesting any and all information they might have on the existence of Mermaids or Merman. What do you think Brandy he ask.

"Are you nuts Robert, our director gave us orders to keep our research secret, not to discuss any of this research with anyone. It is either the beer or too much fresh air

"Robert, sorry dad I am with mother on this one…Jing is interrupted by Robert.

"So how do we get in touch with our colleges and get the information we are seeking about Mermaids." Robert ask.

Jing speaks up and said, "Lets research the internet and contact every scientist that has reported any incident with Mermaids or Mermen in every country. We can report to them we are collecting data under another e mail address. We can tell them we are collage researchers and would welcome any assistance from them in the collection of their reports. This way we don't tell them of our study or actual design goals and this will meet our directors goals of keeping our research secret from everyone." Jing suggest.

"I think that is a great idea, You are really bad." Brandy

smiles, "I will email them soon as we go back to the house." Brandy said.

Should we start looking for these Mermaids Brandy." Robert ask.

"With all the reports of sighting we have read are virtually all over the world. I think we should go to the areas where they might have been seen or reported sighting in the recent past years. You know they tend to live in cold waters as well as warm waters, they swim with whales when they give birth in Mexico and Hawaiian warm waters to Alaska and some tend to live in ancient lakes like Clear Lake northern California. Researchers believe they travel through blow holes from the volcanoes that end at the ocean Big Island, south of Hilo about La Pau Hoe Hoe. There is natural shelf with caves that go under Mona Kea. No boats or divers ever dive there because of boat traffic and the currents. No Great Whites have been seen around any of the islands until 2006 when a Great White was spotted off Maui and of course that is where Tiger Sharks hang out because of all the fish off the reef. Until 2006 not even a tiger shark has been seen around Big Island and the one seen was at the Hilton in Kona in the early morning." Brandy replies with a smile.

"I haven't seen you this excited in a while." Brandy tells Robert.

"Well after reading all the research of the past weeks we know now that there is reports of people seeing what they believe is human like females that have fish parts who swim with dolphins have saved sailors from drowning all over the globe. They have done battle with humans on land and the sea, they are afraid of sharks, they possibly have their own langue with might be Sumerian one of the oldest languish know to man. I want to dive on the Big Island for the truth but I want us to....Robert is interrupted by Brandy.

"I know you want to be cautious and I saw what looked like a Navy investigator talking to the boss today in his office and they looked at me then he closed his office blinds. I think they suspect me of taking up Dr. Mathews research maybe...Brandy is interrupted By Robert.

"I agree, we need to be cautious. I don't think they are on to us but with the Navy you never know. They could put bugs in our house, cars so we need keep our conversation on this subject to our self here at the beach only. If we are reassigned or sent to Guam you know they are on to us." Robert laughs with Brandy and Jing.

Brandy looks around just in case someone is trying to listen to them. Robert looks at Brandy and said.

"I don't think they are hanging out here yet." and Laughs.

"Jing what do you really think about these possible Mermaids living in the ocean for millions of years?" Robert asks.

"I know that according to over a hundred religions the earth was covered in water for a period of time. In Genesis 9 God said "Let the waters under the heavens gather into one place and dry land appear or something like that, anyway I think women and men had to go live in the ocean because of all the things like volcano eruptions and lack of food. When I hold my hand up and look at the webbing between my fingers and toes I know in my heart and mind there are Mermaids out there Dad. You me and Mom are going to discover them. Then we will protect them from the evils of man. Jing replies.

"What do we do ladies if they are killers of man like so many of the research suggest." Robert said.

"Well we need to let our security divers and staff know about this research and the possibility of these Mermaids and Mermen attacking us and them in the water." Jing speaks up.

"I am not afraid of them Dad." Jing said.

"It is not about being afraid Jing, this research will be directed to locate and study and collect information about one of the worlds most elusive creatures, half human and half fish, both female and males that are in all the waters of this world. They have survived thousands of years and could kill any of us. So we need to use extreme caution when and if we encounter them anywhere. Robert concludes.

"Are you guys ready for some food" Brandy ask.

"I going to stay here for a few minutes." Jing replies

"I am ready for another beer." Robert replies.

As they walk towards the beach house Robert glances over to his left and notices a gray color sedan with two men sitting in the car. Robert looks straight forward and tells Brandy.

.

"Look now to your left…" Robert looks at Brandy and she is looking straight at the car.

"No don't look at them, look at the house." Robert smiles.

"You are so dumb Robert, first you tell me to look and I look then you tell me not to look. You would make a horrible spy. Jing laughs out loud and said "That is true Dad.

"Hay do you want to catch some surf, I just noticed some good sets coming in." Robert ask.

"Yes, I will change and be out in a minute. Are you coming Jing. Ask Brandy.

"Jing come on in." Robert motions to her from the Lanai

"What is up Dad." Jing ask.

Walk with me into the board shop I want to show you my new board I am working on." In the board shop, Robert puts his finger over his lips to warn Jing. In a low voice.

"Look out to your right and see that Gray Naval car with two guys in suits just sitting there. They are spying on us to find out what we know about their Mermaid in captivity. Let's go out and talk to your surfing friends ok." Robert ask Jing.

"Lets do it Dad." Jing replies.

All of them change into their swim suits, grab their board and head back out to the beach not looking at the gray sedan parked off the shoulder of the road with the two men looking at them. One of the men is holding what appears to be a hand held voice ampler to listen in on their conversations. As they all paddle out through the surf. Jing and Brandy turn around and look at the sedan and notice the two men are not in the car now, but they can't tell where they are.

The two Navy Investigators ran around to the back of the residence and walked through open back door. Both investigators are astonished at the stacks of research papers, books that now clutter the living room and part of the lanai. Just then Ariel attacks one of the Naval Investigators by biting his ankle, he is screaming and runs out the back door with Ariel hanging on growling. One investigator placed bugs throughout the house. Ariel let go but continued to bark at them but no one could hear her. One investigator walked and the other limped to their car hoping they are not seen by anyone. Now in their car they wait for Robert, Brandy and Jing to return to the house so they can listen to their conversations.

Robert and Brandy have now paddled next the locals made up of younger Hawaiian boys and girls who are friends.

"What's up Robert", Hi Jing, Brandy, nice board is that new." Tommy ask.

"No, I bought it used last week from a Howe who was going back to the mainland for a hundred dollars." Jing tells him.

"Hay I will give you a hundred for it." Tommy tells Jing.

"Not for sale now Tommy, but if I decide to sell it will be yours." Jing smiles.

Jing speaks up. "Hay guys we need your help, these two Howes are parted down the road trying to spy on us. I need you guys to screw with them so they leave."

"We will go catch the next wave while the locals go after the Naval Investigator." Tommy tells them.

Brandy and Jing catch the first wave. Robert follows, they walk up to their house without saying a word. After leaning there boards against the wall in the back and go into the house to change. Brandy looks at Jing and Robert putting his finger across the lips and points at what appears to be a listing device put into one of her plants in the bedroom.

Brandy writes a note to Robert "Those bastards." Jing reads the note and whispers "wait until you see our locals do to them". Robert and Brandy carry on simple conversations about surfing and walk out to the Lanai to watch all the action. As they look at the ocean the local surfers are no where to be seen. Soon the group of surfers appear surrounding gray sedan and they start throwing crabs into the front seat along with seaweed covering the entire inside and outside car. The locals are yelling.

"Get out of here Howes"

The agents are yelling profanities and drive off trying to remove the crab and seaweed from their vehicle. Jing, Robert, and Brandy are laughing and wave to the locals.

The locals return to the surf. Brandy, Jing, and Robert search for the listing devices. After an hour searching they have found several then walk into the lanai to rest and talk about today's events. Jing grabs all the bugs and smashes all of them on the floor with a rock.

"What an afternoon, Do we really need all this stuff, after all we are just researchers not James Bond for God sake." Robert tells Brandy and Jing.

"You are right Robert, but as scientist and researchers we always question everything and seek the truth. What is happening is that some force is trying to stop our search.

"Who are you talking about." Robert ask.

"I am talking about the Navy is trying to stop our research or block it from finding out they have a real Mermaid in tank at one of their bases. They are doing their own research."

"How are you going to convince Dr. Wilson to use all of NOAA's assets to search for a Mermaid in the ocean." Robert ask.

"Did you forget Robert that it was Dr. Wilson who

called us and directed us to do this research." Brandy tells Robert.

"You know Robert that Dr. Wilson has a Hugh ego and if he thinks that this research will get him a Nobel Lariat or a mention in the Journals he will give us an army to search for the facts as he has in the past. Oh I just received an email from the good doctor and we have now been reassigned to the Marine Division. Is that weird or what. Think someone is listing to us." Brandy ask Robert.

"You just may have something Brandy and what we need to do is to write up all the research that has been done already and quantify it in terms of actual sightings by individuals verses researchers with credentials and develop scales, you know how Dr. Wilson likes scales to measure efficacy of the data."

Now assigned to the Marine Division on Oahu both Robert, Brandy and Jing continue their own research while working in secret on the proposal for Dr. Wilson. They return all the books to the libraries and write and develop several hypothesis to test the efficacy of the collected data which turns out to be quit amassing because there are data of sighting shows two or more intervals report sighting from as far back as 200BC. The reporting had been logged into ship Captains logs and fisherman all over the world including deck hands to Navy's' from all contents and oceans. The most significant finding is the drawings in the caves of the plateau in Egypt.

Almost completed with the proposal for Dr. Wilson when Brandy receives a phone call from a colleague from Japan, she reports a Hugh earthquake and fisherman from a local village report some type of fish or person helped all the fisherman from drowning from the tsunami that followed. She read Brandy's email sent last week for data regarding any actual sighting of possible Mermaids. Brandy walks' very fast over to Roberts lab and motions for him to step outside for a moment. Outside Brandy tells Robert along with Jing.

"You will not believe what has happened in Japan…" Robert interrupts her.

"Yes I just heard about the earthquake and tsunami hundreds are missing and…" Brandy interrupts Robert.

"I know Robert but listen to me, one of our colleagues from Tokyo just called me said that a fishing boat overturned outside a village north of them and some type of fish or person saved some of the fishermen and took some of them down, Robert do you think it could be a Mermaid and why would it kill some of them," Brandy ask.

"No one said these things called Mermaids in our ocean were friendly just look at the Reports from all over the world from intervals and in text along with other reports and writings in the middle east countries like Egypt. Ok it is time to get that meeting with Dr. Wilson. I will call his office and see if he has time to see us." "Of course." Robert replies.

Robert calls Dr. Wilson secretary and Dr. Wilson himself hears' his secretary is talking with Robert and he picks up his phone and motions his secretary to hang up.

"This is Dr. Wilson how are you all doing." He ask in old gruffly voice.

"Just fine Dr. Wilson we have a research project we would like you to consider pursuing and…" He is interrupted by Dr. Wilson.

"Just put it in the mail bag today and when I get back

from Japan, I will look at it, I must go now Robert I have to catch a plane now." Dr. Wilson hangs up.

"Just great." Robert said out loud. He calls Brandy and tells her the bad news. Brandy then tells Jing.

"While you have been bullshitting with his highness I got us three seats on a Coast Guard KC130 to Japan, now get your gear and I will meet you at the car." Brandy tells Robert and Jing.

"Oh, I have to call to see if Tu Tu can watch Ariel and your Fat cat", Brandy tell s them. "Alright, we need to be on the tar mat in fifteen minutes." Brandy tells them.

Soon they arrive at the tar mat and park the NOAA Toyota Land Cruiser against the fence. As they get out of the Toyota they run to the KC130 as the props are starting to turn and the ramp is still down in the back. As they run towards the ramp Robert just takes a look around his shoulder as he felt someone following them and he see's those same two Naval suits, now standing at the fence looking at them run up the ramp. As soon as they entered the plane the loadmaster closes the ramp door and they taxi to take off.

Soon they are off heading for Japan. While in the airplane Robert and Brandy and Jing read over the proposal for Dr. Wilson. The load Master walks over to both of them and tells them.

"We just received a message from your director and he wants both of you to meet him inside the Coast Guard hanger in Japan. That's all the message said." The loadmaster smiles and returns to his seat.

As they fly along the coast of Japan they can see the devastation caused by the 7.3 earthquake and the tsunami that has killed thousands and destroyed entire villages along the coast. It was reported that the tsunami was ninety feet high in many areas along the coast, not even a sixty foot sea wall to keep back the tsunami waves. Looking out the plane window it looked like a bomb had exploded, debris everywhere and water everywhere. Soon they land at the coast guard station inland to Tokyo.

They see the director from the windows of the KC130 as it taxies up to the hanger. Soon the rear ramp comes down and Brandy, Jing and Robert walk down the ramp and walk over to Dr. Wilson who is standing next to a new Toyota Land Cruiser with a large NOAA sign on the doors he smiles and said.

"Doctors please get into the Land Cruiser over here." The traffic on the roads is real bad and driving on the wrong side of the road isn't easy, it will take us some time to get to the University for your meeting," Dr. Wilson tells them.

All got into the Toyota without any comment but look at each other in anticipation of the trip. Dr. Wilson is sitting on the front right seat turns around and smiles. Not paying attention to his driving when everyone tells him to pay attention to the traffic.

"I knew what you three are up to for some time now but I could not let any of you know. Naval Intel has been all over us about not pursing looking for dead Mermaids or Dolphins and not reporting our finding to the scientific community or our congress supporters. I know they have been spying on you doctors. Don't you worry we are going to pursue the search for the truth and I will worry about the heat ok." As he looks over at Robert and Jing sitting in the back seat with Jing in the third row seats.

"Right Dr.Wilson, we have started to develop a hypotheses and…" He is interrupted by Dr. Wilson.

"Great and I want you to share all your research with me as we develop and expand the search but we must keep our research and findings very secret from everyone. The reason of course is that the Navy is very protective of their underwater sonar devices and the harm they can do that they will sink anyone's boat who interferes with their research even though they are killing whales, dolphins and possibly Mermaids remains to be seen." Dr. Wilson turns around and gives Brandy and Jing a smile. Now look you two, Naval Intelligence told me that these so called Mermaids can be very deadly. They would not liberate about how they are deadly but warned me to be careful around these subjects so you two I want you to use our divers on any underwater research for these things ok."

Brandy ask. "So how did you know Robert, Jing and me were coming here."

"Naval Intelligence called me and have asked me to report back to them, they have no idea how close all of us are in the scientific community. They look at everything like black and white or Officer and enlisted person." Dr. Wilson turns and smiles at Robert.

"Look all of us are doctors in our respective fields and have one goal together and that is for the truth. Now who are you guys meeting here." Dr. Wilson ask.

"We are meeting Dr. Aika Tanaka from the University of Japan. She has new data about possible Mermaid being caught in a fishermen's net just before the tsunami." Brandy replies.

"Ok, you guys I am going to drop you off at the

University here and you will have to get her to drive you back to the tar mat when you are finished with your investigation, just keep me informed so I can get my Nobel for the research." Dr. Wilson laughs and drops them off at the University Ocean Research laboratory. Inside the University laboratory they meet with Dr. Tanaka. They great each other, exchange business cards and Dr. Tanaka directs them to her office. One of the doctors staff bring in hot tea and Doctor Tanaka said. "There has been some reports that Mermaids have saved many Japanese from the ocean along the coast. As soon as we receive conformation of these acts I will of course share them with you doctors. As I reported to you, we received information directly from the owner of a fishing business. He owns many boats, and a Mermaid grabbed one of his fisherman. We will go and see him in person. First I would like all of you to examine this fingernail recovered from the fishermen that was grabbed. When he was on deck, that thing, half human and fish grabbed him and drugged him into the ocean."

The fisherman fought it off and swam back to the boat. Under his fingernails was the skin of possible Mermaid." Dr. Tanaka said. "We will test the DNA."

"He was the only one who survived the first wave and when he was at his uncle's house here in Tokyo he put the skin that was under his fingernails into this jar and sealed it for us. He actually froze the sample for us. I got the sample yesterday and called you." She said.

"Take a look at the sample and tell me what you think." Dr.Tanaka ask both of them as she steps away from the microscope. Brandy steps up to the microscope and looks for a minute. She raises her head, looks at Robert and said.

"Well Robert what do you see." Robert looks up with a smile and said.

"These are human cells not fish like, do we have any movie or pictures of this thing who attacked the fisherman. Robert ask. Jing speaks up and said.

"Dad let me see." While Jing is looking into the microscope Robert ask.

"Did you get any pictures, doctor."

"No pictures but a movie, one of the deck hands did capture the entire event on his cell phone. One of the deck hands was in the water fighting for his life when this thing… look here and judge for yourself." Dr. Tanaka holds the cell phone and shows all of them the recording the deck hand took. "Some monster with long teeth grabbed him. I also think this sea monster might have been trying to save him." Dr. Tanaka concludes.

"Why do you say that maybe it was trying to save him, didn't he say the thing grabbed him and tried to pull him down into the water not hold him up out of the water." Brandy ask.

"What we need to do is talk to this fishermen at his house. You doctors can interview him yourself ok." Dr. Tanaka answers Brandy.

Soon they are off driving out of the city of Tokyo into the hills overlooking the ocean. Debris floating everywhere, wondering if there are Mermaids swimming out there, as they drive on the winding road, Dr. Tanaka ask all of them.

"How did you guys get involved in this type of inquiry. I know Dr. Wilson usually does not get involved in these type of inquiries." She ask. "You are right Dr. Tanaka he does not like to get into any controversial inquires and especially with other agencies of ours but we have sufficient information this time that may warrant further inquiry by our staff." Robert looks over at Brandy and Jing then smiles. By the way Dr. what does your name mean in Japanese, I know all Japanese names have a special meaning." Jing ask the doctor.

"My first name is Aika and it means love song. My mother told me that she sang a love song to me when I was born after she named me." Dr. Tanaka said.

"You know my country has a long history back thousands of years reporting seeing Mermaids and Mermen in our oceans with thousands of stories so we view each report from the fishermen as a real sighting and question everything they report." Dr. Tanaka reports.

"I know what you guys are thinking, these people also think there is monsters in the ocean like Godzilla and yes we love monster movies but that does not mean we don't question every report, in fact we do and we follow very strict protocols. Like if you see Godzilla run, ha ha, just a little Japanese humor." Dr. Tanaka laughs out loud.

Brandy, Jing and Robert join her in laughter.

"You realize that these Mermaids are not friendly they kill fishermen. In fact we have more reports of attacks on fishermen and even swimmers." Dr. Tanaka reports.

"We have read some reports of attacks on sailors but no reports of killings other than some attempts by Mermaids. Robert responds.

"Have you investigated any of these killings of fishermen Dr. Tanaka." Brandy ask.

"Yes I have Brandy with our Coast Guard investigators and you would be astonished by the results." I will get those files out for you and copy them for you. She tells her.

Dr. Tanaka pulls over to an area off the road and parks her Toyota. They all get out and look at the devastation.

"There is the fisherman's house over on that hillside. He does not speak English and he is very Japanese in tradition you will see. Just take my lead." The doctor said.

Jing, Robert and Brandy all nod their heads

"Look north and you can see the devastation that occurred from the tsunami. It is just awful." Dr. Tanaka said. Everyone agrees.

Dr. Tanaka looks northward with Brandy, Jing and Robert. Soon they are back into the Toyota and on there way to the fishermen's house. Dr.Tanaka drives into this street where a Japanese traditional nice looking home with several cars are parked in front. Beautiful trees and flowers surround the house and one can see the oceans from the upper deck. They are meet at the door by the fishermen Wife. They are invited into his home. They take off their shoes and follow the wife back into a room and are instructed to sit and are served tea by the women. The fishermen owns a fleet of fishing boats and is very well off according to their standards and ours at the current exchange rate. Though he does not speak English but starts to talk to Dr. Tanaka.

Dr. Tanaka tells Brandy, Jing and Robert that the fisherman wants to show them a movie his employee took when loading the catch. The fisherman rang a bell and a women came into the room with a lap top opened and handed it to the fisherman who Dr. Tanaka referred to as Mr. Sato. Soon Jing, Brandy and Robert were watching with amazement. They watched this huge net being brought onto the fishing boat which was over ninety feet long and a crew of eight men. You could tell the camera was being held and the film was very clear. The net landed on the deck, a human like female with fish like scales from the waist down screams at the workers and opens her mouth with very sharp appearing teeth, she has a ridge protruding from the top of her head, webb like hands and straight hair on her head. Her eyes are black and shin gray. She is not easy on the eyes and a normal reaction might be the same as seeing a monster for the first time. As soon as the net hit the deck the Mermaid fought to get to the railing and escapes over the side of the boat. Just then a huge wave maybe sixty feet high hits the boat and all that can be seen is water and debris, the camera is still running. It is just a wonder the cell phone survived the tsunami, Jing commented.

Brandy and Jing look at Robert and then Dr. Tanaka Mr.Sato is without comment. She is shocked by the film. She knows it is real. There was so much human type behaviors and fish like movements. One has to ask themselves the question why would a very rich fishing boat owner spend the money to fake a Mermaid coming onto his boat. Brandy answers herself he did not fake this movie. It is a real Mermaid. Brandy looks at Dr. Tanaka and ask.

"According to Mermaids myths, legends and lore by author Skye Alexander that Japan and China view Mermaids as elegant, wise, and gifted who live in our oceans, lakes and rivers. Their tails are snake like or fish like and some of them swim with dragons. They also bring good luck to fisherman." Brandy concludes.

Aw Mr.Sato replies, "The Japanese Kappa are frightful water demons that have dragged children under water and devoured them or have helped farmers with their irrigation and doctor set bones. We believe a bit of both perhaps and perhaps that is what happened to me in the bay." He then tells Brandy, Jing, Robert and Dr. Tanaka.

"Do you think that Mr.Sato could point out where he dropped his nets in the oceans before the wave hit them and where he brought them up." Brandy ask.

Dr.Tanaka ask Mr. Sato in Japanese and he rolls out a marine map and points to the area in the South China Sea about twenty miles north of Tokyo harbor and ten miles east of the islands. He looks up at Jing, smiles then Brandy and Robert with a very serious look and speaks, "If you three go into the water looking for the Kappa be very careful these demons are real and they will drag you down into the deep and devour you. The only reason I got away is I fought for my life with my fish knife and I cut it many times. Be careful all of you." As he nods his head. I lost five of my men to them.

The sliding door opens which signals them the meeting is over with and they are lead out of the room to the front door.

As they get into the Toyota and head down the mountain they all look out to the ocean and take a minute to reflect on the fisherman's warnings.

Robert said. "You know that the stargazer fish has a face like Mr. Chin described, looks like human at a glance, sharp teeth, very aggressive with poison spins on his back and 50 volts hides in the sand..." He is interrupted by Brandy.

"No one could mistake a Mermaid for a Stargazer, they are indeed ugly." and they all laugh. Jing speaks up and said.

"I went out on a blind date one time who looked like a Stargazer." They all again laughed. Brandy ask Robert. Where do we go now guys." Dr.Tanaka ask.

"I have been thinking, All of us should write something about what we heard and saw today. I would like your opinion about everything including you Jing. I suspect that there are only small pods of these Mermaids because of what mankind has done to our waters around the world. For example...

"Oh we are here at my office, lets go inside it is cold outside and lo**ok at the** debris in the bay, it is just horrible." Dr.Tanaka concludes.

Inside the Doctors office she continues.

"Here are copies of my research for all of you." She said.

"Between July 16, 1945 and September 23 1992 your country has conducted 1054 nuclear test. Now this is why there are only a hand full of these water persons left, I call your attention to this list of test since the two dropped on my country." Dr.Tanaka eyes fills with tears. Robert, Brandy and Jing look at each other. Brandy reaches out to Dr. Tanaka to stroke her arm.

"The nuclear test just conducted in our oceans by your country, not including all the other countries, You guys just look at this list. No wonder there are only a few Mermaids left and they are angry with us humans." Dr.Tanaka continues as she reads from a book with tears in her eyes. "Listen to this." She continues. "I hand out this informal information sheet that was written by a researcher for the world to see that in 1956 our government stepped up the testing at the Bikini Atoll and the Enewetak Atoll 17 Atmospheric test were conducted in 1958 another 35 atomic test were conducted in the atmosphere over the Bikini Atoll, Enewetak Atoll and Johnson Island in the south Pacific. Then in 1962 Christmas Island, Johnson Island and Central

Pacific experienced 36 nuclear test of 150 kt. Bombs or less over the islands. The majority of Nuclear testing was conducted at Nellis Air Force Range, Nevada test sight, New Mexico test sight, Mississippi, Aleutian Islands off the coast of Alaska. No effort was made by any agency to test the effects on your own population until 15 years later. I think maybe your country had more deaths from cancer than we may have had from the two bombs dropped on our country. Anyway, I am sorry for all the Mermaids and Mermen and families that have been killed by all the nuclear testing and nets dragged in the oceans and the old fishes killed for sport. Not to mention plastic containers thrown into water ways without regard for the creatures who live in those waters. So what do you both think." Dr Tanaka concludes, all this information is printed for the public and history.

Brandy speaks up. "I had no idea it was that many, I am so shocked and certainly have a new outlook for these Mermaids." Jing speaks up. "Me too Mom."

"I had no idea." Robert replies just looking at all the ladies.

Sitting around the conference table drinking tea, water and diet Pespi, Brandy speaks up and said.

"There is more I need to tell all of you. My research on these Mermaids has taken me too.

After reading Dr. Mathews research and interviewing Japanese who reported seeing these Mermaids, and my additional research with my staff, and we believe that most of the Mermaids that are left on earth are hiding in lava tubes around the pacific rim. Now I will tell you why. We have literally thousands of reports for centuries from all over the word about intervals seeing, contacting Mermaids and Mermen but during the period from World War 11 until the end of the Vietnam War there has not been one recording of anyone seeing any Mermaids. Now we know that the warm waters of the Pacific Coast are preferred buy fish during this time of the year. Dr. Mathews said… "Dr. Brandy Walters is interrupted by Dr. Tanaka staff as they walk into the room.

"Oh doctors this is my staff." She said and orders her staff to take a seat. "You guys have a seat." They all sit around the conference table that face the ocean with floor to ceiling windows. The staff had brought in Japanese bread cakes and more cold soda drinks. Tanaka introduces her young staff and informs Brandy, Jing and Robert they all speak English. "Ok, lets get started, I was just telling your Doctor Tanaka of why we believe the Mermaids have left other areas of the ocean and retreated to hiding places that still give them access to the waters, fish and nutrients. When mankind started testing Atomic Bombs, not just in the Pacific waters but the Russians, North Korea, Pakistan and China the Mermaids and Mermen, their children, headed for safer waters. We believe that 90% of all the are hiding and living in lava tubes around the Pacific Rim where contently 90% of the Volcano are located. For example the Ai-La'au Pahoehoe flow that erupted in 1859 from the 11,000 foot level entered Kiholo Bay 32 miles away of the Hawaii Islands. The best is yet to come. Tommy tell the doctors what you and the staff found in the lava tube off the Big Island of Hawaii. Dr. Tanaka ask.

"Yes", Tommy responds, "While traveling through the lava tube about a mile into the tube we found hiding in a crack in the wall spears and rock arrow heads just like Dr.

Mathews describes and that fishermen have recovered. We all went to the end of it but the tube goes into the water in the bay so someone…Dr. Tanaka interrupts Tommy,

"Ok Tommy thank you."

"We think our first search should be underwater in Kiholo Bay, there are no Tiger Sharks around the Big Island they are always around Maui because of the shelf and fish and we know the Mermaids do not like sharks." concludes Dr. Tanaka

Dr. Tanaka stops talking for a minute then ask Brandy, Jing and Robert what they think of her proposal. Robert looks at Brandy and Jing, takes the lead as he is the senior scientist.

"Well I like the proposal, but we will have to run this buy our boss and the state department. I think it is very doable for all of us to work together in the search for the truth and knowledge." Robert concludes. Brandy speaks up.

"I agree with Robert and after all the research you and your staff have conducted on this matter it is to our mutual interest that we all work together. Now you mentioned that you think these Mermaids have left the oceans swimming with dolphins and whales to hide in lava tubes and only coming out of them to fish." Brandy looks at Dr. Tanaka "Yes, if they sun bath like in the past they must do it very carefully. My Staff recommended we search lava tubes around the Pacific Rim that reach the ocean in search for Mermaids and Mermen pods of them hopefully. From the south Pacific, New Zealand, up the Pacific Coast countries to north of San Francisco where there is a lava tube that comes from Mt. Konocti in Lake County which is a very interesting place.

As Dr. Tanaka points to a map, her assistant have put up on a stand. We will then go up the coast of California, Oregan, where there are several interesting lava tubes that go into the Pacific Ocean and Washington State, up to Alaska. I think we should pass on the Aleutian Islands that is where Atomic test were conducted and I doubt there are any live Mermaids." comments or suggestions Dr. Brandy, Jing, Robert?"

"Not right now, Ladies." Robert replies.

Jing speaks up. "How long have you and your staff have been researching Mermaids doctor."

"Jing, we have been researching Mermaids and their behaviors over the last fifty-three years. I have been researching them personally for the last five years. We have collected data from all over the world. We will share all our data with you doctors and of course we would like to review your data also." Doctor Tanaka concludes.

"You can count on it Doctor.Tanaka Robert replies.

"Thank you all for the assistance and we will be in touch soon. But right now we need someone to drive us back to the tar mat so we can catch a plane back to Oahu." Robert again replies.

"I can do that." Dr. Tanaka replies.

While driving back to the airbase by one of the doctors students, Brandy glances over at Doctor Tanaka who is sitting next to her and Jing in the back seat of the Toyota and ask.

"Dr. How did you learn about all these lava tubes around the rim of fire, this would take years...Brandy is interrupted by Dr. Tanaka

"This information was gathered many years ago by our

fishermen, they would take small boats off the big boat and get close to the coast and dive for different types of shell fish and during these dives they discovered the lava tubes going into the ocean. The Captain. would log these findings and my staff researched the old logs and now we have that data to explore for the Mermen and Mermaids. The Dr. smiles over at Brandy and Jing.

Brandy looks at Robert and smiles then replies to Dr. Tanaka

"Great data, we will be in touch with you as soon as we meet with our boss ok. I hope the earth quake and Tsunami did not have any effect on our air base." Brandy said.

"My staff called ahead for you doctors and the air base and tar mat is ok. We will be waiting for your call." The Dr. say goodbye and get on the plane.

On board the Air force KC 130 plane flying back to Oahu Brandy ask Robert and Jing "So what is your take of the interview and Dr. Tanaka proposal to search for the Mermaids with us. Brandy raises her voice to over come the roar of the plans engines.

"Well I was impressed with the Captain and owner of the fishing fleet and his first hand observation of what seems to be some type of half fish and half human women. I also have to acknowledge the Japanese are years ahead of us in our research for the truth about these Mermaids." Robert replies smiling at Brandy and Jing.

"I noticed you just change your attitude towards these Mermaids or Mermen." Brandy looks at Robert and smiles.

"Well when you see for yourself that they could be relatives of ours perhaps even the missing link between the Neanderthal and Homo sapiens. I now think that when the earth was covered by water like it says in the bibles perhaps man and women entered the oceans to survive like Dr. Mathews suggest. Over millions of years they have mutated parts of there bodies to live among the creature of the oceans and lakes. We find new fish species every week around the world. This is very exciting and not to mention very dangerous according to Mr. Chin." Robert laughs and looks at Brandy and Jing.

As they arrive in Oahu they are meet at the tarmac by their boss Dr. Wilson is motioning for them to come over to his SUV Toyota Inside the Toyota Dr. Wilson said.

"I hear the Japanese want to do this research about Mermaids with both of you." Dr. Wilson ask.

.

Robert speaks up, "Eh that's right doctor, Dr. Tanaka proposed that we…" he is interrupted by Dr. Wilson. "I already heard from my counter-part The ministration of Ocean research a real nice guy, anyway our State Department and Homeland Security want us to go ahead with research with the Japanese government but it has to be kept completely secret from the public ok." He stated looking at Brandy and Robert and glancing at Jing.

"Brandy ask. "Why the secrecy doctor."

"The reason is Brandy that if the general public were to know that real Mermaids were in our waters and they posed a danger to our communities, beach goers, suffers boaters and we did not warm them and they could and most likely panic and can cause more harm than good. We would not be able to protect them from the public. This data cannot be shared with anyone understand." Dr. Wilson concludes.

"Yes doctor, Yes doctor." both Brandy and Robert answer." Ok" answers Jing.

"Oh buy the way, Naval Intelligence has a report for you both to read about Mermaids and the only one they captured and why it died, so call their office and ask for Agent Billings." Dr. Wilson said.

"I am going to drop you two off at your Toyota and make sure you type up your report tonight and meet me in my office at 10am tomorrow for a meeting. Ok you guys see you both tomorrow." The Dr. said.

"See you tomorrow." Robert tells Dr. Wilson.

Inside their new Toyota on the high way to north shore Brandy, Robert and Jing finally relax as Robert drives pass Hickem Field and both of them look at each other and just smile holding each others hand for a moment in time. Without a word said they know that they love each other and no word or group of words can replace the internal thoughts each of them have of love for the other.

"No matter where we go Robert I am bringing Ariel with us, I just can't stand being without her." Brandy tells Robert and Jing.

"Ok, I agree I miss Ariel too." Jing replies and smiles.

"We can't bring Fat cat because he will go overboard." Brandy tells Robert.

"He will not, I am bring him with us, he is my cat and I am not leaving him behind, besides he can chase rats on board the ship." Robert replies.

That cat of yours is such a pussy the rats will probably eat him, ok if I can bring Ariel you can bring Fat Cat." Brandy replies.

Meanwhile they arrive at home and are greeted by Ariel

and Fat Cat with love on the Lanai. Brandy pays Tu Tu and she tells Ariel and Fat cat "good buy."

"Ok tell me what you think about this possible adventure around the ring of fire in search for Mermaids." Brandy ask everyone.

"Well if you get me a beer I will be able to answer you." Robert responds with a smile.

"Ok darling, but I really want to talk to you and Jing about is this trip." Brandy answers.

"Thank you for the cold one Brandy." Robert still smiling.

"Ok me first. This search for Mermaids around the ring of fire could be easily the find of the century for science. Since we can not tell anyone or write a book about the search we can document the entire search into a significant paper for science. What do you think guys." Jing concludes.

"Wow, Jing that was impressive, yes I agree." Robert said.

"Me to Jing, we will keep detail notes everyday on everything so we can write that paper." Brandy said.

"Alright, I think we all. I mean the agency and our colleges from Japan are heading in the right direction on this Mermaid issue. For example we need to know how many Mermaids are out there, how many pods and where they are, so we can protect them from the public and care for them as we do all mammals in the oceans." Robert concludes. Now looking at Brandy and Jing with a serious face.

"I agree with your position but I think we need to have some type of agreement from our colleges government that they will agree to the same things our government agencies will do to protect the Mermaids, remember they signed an agreement about the whales and under the guise of research they still kill them and eat them." Brandy responds, drinking her beer and petting Jack.

That agent Billings for the report on the captured Mermaid Robert." Brandy tells Robert.

"It would be ok but today is Friday at 6pm and everyone is gone for the weekend, so lets catch some surf, eat some fish and a salad, and we can talk about desert later." Robert replies smiling."

"You guys are sick." Jing said. Robert smiles and looks at Brandy as she heads out to the surf watch. Sounds great darling, lets get our boards." Brandy said.

Robert smiles and looks at Brandy. Brandy heads around the back with Robert and they get their surf boards and head out to the surf. The air is so clear one could eat it if it were food and the warm air just makes your skin feel good like an afternoon in a slight warm air with a slight wind that you just want to curl up and go to sleep.

As they enter the water in the bay Brandy's long blond hair glows against the sun and Robert turn to his side and just looks at her for a moment in time and realizes how lucky he is with this beautiful women and a doctor to butte. Fat cat is laying on Ariel on the sofa asleep knowing his buddy is back home for now.

As Brandy and Robert sit on their boards waiting for a good set to come in Robert ask Brandy. "Hay babe, what do you think about going on the Japanese ship that has been used as a whaling ship in the recent past, the so called research of whales...Robert is interrupted by Brandy and Jing.

"I will not step one foot on that boat." Jing said. "Me

too Jing, I am not going on that ship, there are dead whale spirits on that ship, bad mojo. What do you think honey." Brandy ask.

"Here comes a good set, you go first Jing, You take the next one babe." Robert tell Brandy.

Robert heads his board towards the break and gets on top of the wave, his board is a ten 0, just riding the board is fun without any cut backs. It is what we do when reach an age. Brandy waited and caught the wave of the day as Robert watches her ride the wave through the tube. They drag their boards into the yard and take a shower outside.

"Lets have a beer and discuss how we are going to approach the boss about not using the Japanese ship for research but use our own research ship."

"Good idea, babe, how we are going to approach the boss, I hate that, he can be so controlling and….Brandy is interrupted by Jing.

"Hay he is the boss and he is controlling we all agree, so lets give him something to take control of. Just ask him if he wants his scientist being controlled by the Japanese on their research vessel. Remember the story he told us about his father was captured and tortured by the Japanese in the Philippines on some death march. Do you really think he will allow that to happen. We need to discuss how we might handle this matter as it might cause a problem between our countries, what do you think." Jing concluded.

"Some times Jing shocks me with all the right answers, man you are smart." Robert tells Jing.

"You are smart Jing." Brandy said.

"Thanks guys." Jing replies.

"Well, I think we should have a meeting with the boss on Monday and….." Brandy is interrupted by Robert.

"We just got an e mail from the boss and he wants us in his office at 8am Monday for a meeting. So your wish came true. As Robert laughs. Brandy smiles at Robert and Jing as if she had just sent a telegraphic message to the boss as she looks out at the waves braking and the sunset.

Monday morning at NOAA headquarters offices Dr. Wilson is waiting in the conference room for Doctors Robert and Brandy and Jing. Brandy notices there are at lease twenty chairs set up with place sitting and fresh fruit, Hawaiian bread alone with bottle of water on the table.

"So what is this all about Dr. Wilson." Brandy ask.

"We are going to have a meeting this morning with State Department Officials, Naval Intel and other government personnel. This Mermaid documentary has caught the attention of many of our agencies and some government officials'. So I suggested we have this meeting so we can all get on the same page as you both know our goal is to find out where they live about how many there are in our oceans and lakes and protect them from the public and our own government agencies namely the Navy Soniar testing project. Our meeting starts at 9am so I want to get our position tightened up between us right now and we will stay with it during the meeting. Ok doctors. So please take a seat. I have a list of our policy's and procedures here so I would like to hear from each of you on area's of concern and what you want to see happen in this upcoming voyage with the Japanese." Dr. Wilson looks towards the telephone and said.

"Dr. Mathews how is the weather in South Africa." Dr.

Wilson smiles and looks at Robert, Brandy and Jing as they all smile.

"Hot, very hot thank you Dr. Wilson I appreciate being part of this meeting and hello to you doctors Brandy and Robert and our newest inter Doctor Jing soon."

"So are you going to come on this expedition with us doctor." Robert ask.

"Yes I am, are you kidding I would not miss this one for the world, this is my life's goal and…. Dr. Mathews is interrupted by Dr. Wilson.

"Ok guys, lets get started, Dr. Mathews what are your concerns with the other agencies. Dr. Wilson ask Dr. Mathews.

"My concern is that the Navy will continue with their testing and kill off the rest of the Mermaids not to mention hundreds of whales. I also don't like the idea of doing research on a Japanese Ship. All of you know that there so called research ship is used in killing whales. They lie and tell us it is for research but they take the carcass directly to the market for sale. We have that documented. I don't want interference with other countries in our research along shores or lakes. I don't want any interference from our own Navy. Those are my concerns doctors." Dr. Mathews said.

"Ok doctors, that sums it up at lease for me, what are your concerns Doctors Walters, Brandy, Jing, Robert" Dr. Wilson ask.

"Well I share Dr. Mathews concerns and I would like some assurances from our Navy that their research will stop until we complete our research. I would like our State Department to contact all the officials ahead of us and gain their support in our research without them really knowing what we are researching for so we can be left alone to do our jobs around the ring of fire. Brandy replies.

"Ok, Robert what are your concerns, that the Japanese will eat Fat Cat." Everyone laughs…." Robert is shocked then laughs.

"Come on Robert, you are thinking of Vietnam, not Japan, they only eat whales. They are not going to eat Fat Cat we will make sure there boat does not get to close to ours because I have scheduled our ship Hi ialakai, now in Pearl Harbor waiting for all three of you along with our divers and intern scientist. She is 224 feet long and travels at 11 knots. She has rooms for twenty four crew including six officers and twenty two scientist. I have reserved officers rooms for you three which are very nice and your other family members are welcome aboard. You doctors know that this ship of ours' is a oceanographic research ship and she has multiyear sonar and echo sounder equipment for underwater mapping and there are large lockers for all your scientific gear. While you doctors were surfing all weekend me and my staff meet with State Department Officials and they immediately said they did not want us on the Japanese ship and to use our own ship. Next they need a list of ports, the ship can stay at sea for fifty days but we need to know where you will be so we can send our own tanker and keep our ship filled with fuel. and….Doctor Wilson is interrupted by Brandy.

"Doctor Wilson when we refuel what about food and supplies."

"Good question, at forty days I will have all the food and supplies put on the tanker and transported to your ship while refueling. That way no one will get sick like in the past by eating what the natives eat." Dr. Wilson said.

"Ok I need to inform you doctors about one caveat of this research project and this comes down from the highest level of government and you know what that means." Dr. Wilson smiles.

"That caveat is that this research is classified secret and none of the information collected will be shared with anyone other than your Japanese counterparts. The rational for this secrecy is that we now know there are Mermaids or officially referred to as the M file.

The Navy research team believes Dr. Mathews theory that these Mermaids or early humans had no other choose but to start living in our waters all over the world due to floods and volcanoes eruptions for thousands of years and have evolved into what we refer to as Mermaids and Mermen with a great deal of suffocation and we must protect these species at all cost from the rest of the world as we all know they would be exploded and we would lose again another species and a possible relative of ours." Dr. Wilson concludes and holds his head down in worry.

Jing rubs Dr. Wilson's back with one hand and tells him.

"Don't worry, we will find this species and then we can set up the protection of these Mermaids. In order for us to study them we must be able to protect them. They can be so aggressive at times. They even use weapons to attack there foes. We must convince them we will not harm them and…" Jing is interrupted by Dr. Mathews.

"How do we do that when our own Navy is testing sonar that kills them and their friends, dolphins and whales…" he is interrupted by Dr. Wilson

"The Navy has assured me that their research will stop until our research is concluded and I have that assurance from the Admiralty. All we can do is our best and believe and question everything as we do. Also the Navy is going to share all there research with us regarding the Mermaids they have recovered and all pathology. The Navy scientist are also going to share what knowledge they have about some of the dangers in handling these species. It is 08:55 and we need to get ready for this meeting with the Navy and State Department. Write down any questions so we cover everything doctors.

It is 9:00 am and the Naval officers show up wearing their white uniforms. The room is full of anticipation of negative attitudes that the doctors are expecting to come from the Navy. The doctors just stare at the Naval Officers. No smiles are exchanged and soon several men and women arrived from the State Department they are all wearing visitor badges issued by the security guards as you enter the building. The men are wearing summer suits no tie and all three of them have short Marine type hair cuts. The two women are wearing pant suits in a very conservative cut with their hair put into a bun. Both of the women wear glasses and sit next to each other.

"Will everyone please find a seat, help yourself to the refreshments and we will get started." Dr. Wilson ask.

Soon everyone takes a seats with their coffee and fruit. They are all seating at a long conference table like in a board room, but this conference room is in the inland water ways of Perl Harbor over looking NOAA Ships and the Officers golf course in the distant view with palm trees. Dr. Wilson sips on his water and starts the meeting. "Alright we are all here to discuss our research of Mermaids. This research is unlike or untaken by NOAA ever. Our mission is to locate this spies known to all of us as Mermaids. We all now know that this mission is a secret one. Though there has been literally thousands of reporting's of Mermaids all over the world, no one has ever captured one except our Navy. I have been informed that that Mermaid is dead.

"Is that correct Commander." Dr. Wilson ask.

"Yes it is Dr. Wilson." The Commander replies.

For the protection of these species in the ocean and our water ways when we locate them we must keep their habit and information about them from the public to protect this species or they will surely be taken advantage of by humans seeking monetary gains. I would like to hear now from the Navy on this subject. Commander." Dr. Wilson concludes.

"Thank you Dr. Wilson I am Commander Schultz from Naval Intel. Yes the Navy had one of these species in our possession for about three months. I have a complete report from our scientist on this species and our complete study. The purpose of our study was to determine if this species was a threat us or we could use this species for underwater research. We concluded neither. This species of part human and part fish, you will read in the report that their DNA is the same as ours. This species evolved much like Dr. Mathews suggested in his 2009 report to the Senate that during a period when our earth was covered in water our species entered the waterways to survive and they did so over millions of years. They have a special ability to communications with other mammals

.

For that reason we have stopped all testing of sonar

throughout the world until it is safe for this species if ever. Our scientist are standing by for you and your staff Dr. Wilson to examine and take this species into your lab for further research and analysis.

We want to assist NOAA in this research of the pacific rim in search of these species by offering our Navy Seals as divers to protect your scientist from this species. It has been our experience that this species is very aggressive and tends to attack any intruders and kill or maim any other species that enter there domain." Any questions, Thank you again." Commander Schultz concludes looks around the table for anyone asking questions.

Jing sitting across from the Commander speaks up.

"Commander Schultz what guarantee do we have that the Soniar testing will stop, not only in the Pacific but all over the world." Jing ask.

"We are stopping all testing in the Pacific Ocean as of one week ago, however the Navy will continue working with our partners on Soniar dection in the Medriation and other ocean areas and you are?" The Commander ask with a frawn on his face.

"Commander Schultz I am Jing Walters." She replied with a smile on her face as she has got the truth out of the Navy. They plan on continuing their Soniar testing.

"I too was informed that the Navy was going to stop all testing everywhere and that means everywhere Commander, that is according to my sources at the White House. You can be assured I will get to the bottom of this issue before we depart on this research. Ok, this meeting is ended until I get some answers and straighten out this issue. If we are going to protect these Mermaids and Merman it must be in all waters all over the world.

Commander if you kill off our own species of thousand years in other oceans what makes you think that such acts won't drive our Pacific Rim Mermaids into even deeper hiding places. The continuing testing of such Soniar could have a profound effect on the Mermaids all over the world Commander." Dr. Wilson concludes.

Without a word everyone leave the conference room except doctors Brandy, Robert and Jing along with Dr. Walters and Mathews sitting at the conference table.

"Well that was very informative. All of us here have the same view and goals and that is to understand this species, protect them where needed from our species

"Good job Jing, you got that old goat to tell the truth. You just saved the lives of many Mermaids and Mermen. "Great Dr.Wilson said.

Dr. Mathrews spoke up and said. "Well I need to get back to South Africa doctors and try and protect the Mermaids and Mermen from our Navy. Are you ok with that Dr." He ask Dr. Walters."excellent Dr. Mathews, go right ahead and we will meet up with you in a few months. I will keep you in the loop with our research. Soon Dr. Mathews leaves the conference room.

Jing ask Dr. Wilson, "What is the State Department role with our research doctor." She ask.

"The State Departments interest is two run interference for NOAA from each country ahead of your research and we will provide a cover story to protect the integrity of the research. As all of you now know that this research is now classified and nothing we talk about in this room is to shared with anyone. The Navy of course can share what they determine is need to know for the Navy Seals. Also our research department agrees with NOAA position with regards to the protection of the Orcas, that these killer whales have their own language, food sources and don't interbreed with other killer whales and we believe this to be true of the species you are seeking." He concludes.

"What is the Japanese part in this research." Brandy ask.

"Yes the Japanese have agreed to our view on the confidentiality our project and they will participate with our scientist in that we will share most of our findings but nothing of the Navy's former goals or intelligence of having captured species. Other than that we will work with them." Dr. Wilson concludes.

Dr. Wilson is the Navy going to bring their own ship for the Navy Seals to guard us. Robert ask.

"Yes they are bring their own ship. We do not want them on our ship." He said.

"The more ships we have in the area it might scare off the species, we are already having two ships and any military ships might worry the natives also." Robert replies.

"That is a good point Robert." Dr. Wilson replies.

Brandy looks at Robert and smiles and takes a drink of water as if she is sitting on the little stool between rounds with the big boys.

"Dr. Wilson speaks up "The Navy has ships that are completely undercover as they look just like a working fishing boat or luxury boats that are equipped to do anything. The Navy will bring one of them and following at some distance so we will not interfere with our research ok. The Navy interest is in our research if these creatures are the possible missing link or even part or human. The President herself wants the answer to that question as our research could have a tremendous impact on the world religions. Needless to say your research could affect the entire world at some point and that is why the Navy wants to assist NOAA and all our research. It is absolute imperative we all keep all this research secret from the rest of the world at this time."

"Robert you have indicated that your research shows that you folks believe the Mermaids now live on old volcanic caves where they would have protection from the sharks, humans and still be able to breath and hunt for fish and protect themselves from their enemies. Is that correct." Dr. Wilson said."Yes all the volcano around the ring of fire of the pacific coast. To have any success on search for Mermaids it will be around the blow holes made by the vacones themselves, this is where we think they will be living." Robert concludes.

Brandy whispers to Robert. "Did you suggest these Volcanoes with him."

No did you, how did he know where we wanted to go. Big Island is first on the list and…." Brandy stops and she catches Dr. Wilson looking at her.

"Dr. Wilson I think going to the Big Island first with all our ships will cause to much attention and we have no recent reports of any Mermaids around the island at this time.

"I think the Island of Aogashima 222 miles off of Japan in the Philippine Ocean. We do have recent reports of Mermen and Mermaids at this island. The encounters are in the material Robert has handed out for us review. I think the Japanese will get behind this." Brandy said.

"I will call and make all the arraignments with the

Japanese if we are all in agreement." Dr. Wilson concludes. Are there objections, hell their isn't anyone here now, they all laugh. Alright if there are no more questions we are to sail at 0700 hrs. Friday."

Dr. Wilson concludes as Brandy and Robert look out into Pearl Harbor wondering what they may encounter. What will these Mermaids look and act like.

"While going home do you want to stop and buy some pokie to have with our beer." Brandy ask Robert who is driving.

"Yes that sounds great." Robert replies.

"How do you think the boss got all that information where we wanted to search for without the cooperation of Dr.Hamaski and why would she not call us and let us know about that conversation…." Robert interrupts Brandy.

"It is likely he has communicated with her boss in Japan and she told her or him that she wanted to start right here. Who cares as long as we get the suite for our kids, Fat Cat and Ariel, right my love." Robert smiles.

Brandy looks over at Robert and smiles, "Right especially Ariel."

Brandy and Robert drive to the research ship docked in Perl Harbor. Fat Cat is in Roberts back pack and Ariel is in Brandy's arms. They unloads suitcases and research equipment. Brandy looks over at Fat Cat and smiles as she holds onto sleepy Ariel her dog as they walk up the gang plank onto the ship. Soon they are underway heading for an island in the south pacific, part of the Japanese islands, northeast of China. As there ship heads towards the shipping lanes and can no longer be seen from shore the ship changes course abruptly. Brandy and Robert in there cabin feel the turn of the ship and both of them without a word to each other head up the stairs to the bridge. As Brandy, Jing and Robert look around on the bridge they are meet with their boss Dr. Wilson, the Captain and State department personnel.

"Ok you doctors, we are heading for the Big Island area. I know we said that the first island we were going to investigate was one of the Japanese island but there is a Hugh storm heading that way so we decided to investigate the sightings reported to the Navy and …"

"What reports." ask Robert.

"We haven't had the time to copy you on these reports but they seem very plausible Doctors, the State Department personnel hands Roberts the report. Roberts looks at Brandy and Jing then the his boss and said.

"Ok, thank you for this we will bring ourselves up to date." Robert, Brandy and Jing leave the bridge, walk to their cabin. In the room they share the report and read each page without comment, but looking at each other for some comment. Brandy speaks up first, "Well, the first report came from local surfers north of Hilo, I guess that was the first sighting. What does your report say honey." Brandy said "This page covers the second and third sightings. Listen to this, two women that looked like Mermaids were spotted at the county park buy fishermen, you know the park, it is where the soma came in and killed all the children attending school and…" When Robert is interrupted by Brandy.

"I know where the park is, you and I attended the hula contest their, anyway it is a beautiful place to go on the Big Island. If our ladies are living around that area it must be safe for them and their families because no Tiger sharks have been spotted around the island in years." Brandy concludes.

"You are right, Honey I have been told this by many of the locals." Lets find out who is diving and lets get our wet suits on so we can dive with them. I think the area around the park would be a good place to start looking for Mermaids and their families as there are plenty of place to hide around the ref around the island. What do you think Jing" Ask Robert.

"I agree, lets head back to the bridge and see what's happening." Jing replies. On the bridge there boss smiles as Brandy, Jing and Robert enter.

"Ok you three do you want to dive with our Seals." Dr. Wilson ask.

"Yes, most defiantly." Brandy replies.

"Ok you three remember these Mermaids have been very aggressive with anyone coming in contact with them in the past. They have weapons capable of killing sharks and even though they appear to be human, they are not or at lease they are different from us and could be very dangerous. Let the Seals do their job and…" Brandy interrupts Dr. Wilson.

"What is there job exactly, Dr. Wilson. Brandy ask.

"It is to keep you three safe and to look and observe and report any activity to me and their Commander, I will notify the other agencies." Dr. Wilson replies.

"So what is our goal here, or what is the plan if we actually come in contact with the Mermaids." Brandy ask Dr. Wilson.

"I don't have an answer for you Brandy, we have to locate them see how many there are of them and see if we can co exists with them, I mean we have a whole slew of questions to answer before any decisions or at lease recommendations can be made.

As I said before this research mission is to gain knowledge by recording, abserving any and all Mermaids or Merman we encounter. Based upon that information we can recommend how we might protect the Mermaids from the profit tears of our societies." I think that might answer your question Dr. Brandy". "Thank you Doctor." Brandy replies.

Robert looks at Dr. Wilson and smiles as Brandy, Jing and Robert leave the bridge again. Jing, Brandy and Robert walk on to the deck and lean on the railing to get a breath of fresh Hawaiian air.

"look at the aft, the Navy Seals must really think that these Mermaids are a danger to our oceans or even national security." Robert comments.

"I think your right Robert but if one of them get on our boat we can always feed them

Fat Cat and…" Brandy is interrupted by Robert.

"Very funny my dear, I think Ariel could shed some pounds." Robert replies.

"Not funny Dad, while I am think about it I am going to get Ariel and walk her on the aft deck and see if he goes poo." Jing said.

While Jing is walking Ariel on the aft deck something in the ocean makes a large splash and several large fins can be seen swimming towards the boat. Jing grabs Ariel as she leans over the railing to get a better look at whatever is swimming towards the boat.

As Jing looks over the railing she can see what appears to be several Mermaids swimming very fast under the boat.

Brandy also sees the Mermaids and yells out to Robert who is also looking at the port side of the boat and smiles at Brandy.

"Did you see that Robert." Ask Brandy.

"I sure did." Robert yells out.

"How about you Jing, what do you think." Robert ask.

"I can't believe what I saw Dad, they are real, really alive but really ugly or even scary Dad." Jing comments.

"Well maybe if you had to live in the ocean for millions of years you might not look so great either." Robert replies with a smile.

Robert walks over to Brandy with a big smile on his face.

"Can you believe what just happened, we actually viewed a pod of Mermaids swimming towards the Big Island." Brandy tells Robert.

"Yes I can babe, I got a movie of them on my cell phone for proof guys." We need to notify the boss right now." Robert replies.

"Really Robert wonder if the Navy Seals are here to kill them or even if….Brandy is interrupted by Robert.

"Look, we have too, we agreed with everyone that we would share our findings, so lets notify the boss right now." Robert tells Brandy and Jing.

"Alright, let's do it." Brandy said

Robert and Brandy go and meet with Dr. Wilson in the chart room. They both tell what they just observed and show him the cell phone video. Dr. Wilson claps his hands in delight and said.

"I can't believe you got this on film. This is the proof we need of Mermaids guys. You have done it. What luck and good move Robert having your cell phone right there at the right moment in time.' I am so proud of you guys."

He thanks all three them and starts notifying other department heads. Jing went back to her cabin with Ariel as Brandy and Robert walk out of the Chart room feeling somewhat perplexed at the attitude of Dr. Wilson not telling them what was going to happen next or what plans are now going to be put into motion to view, count and learn the habits behaviors of the Mermaids human and half fish.

As Brandy and Robert leave the Chart room they again walk out onto the port side of the boat. At the railing Brandy's attention is now focused on two combat rubber raiding craft also know as a CRRC which is a special fabricated rubber inflatable rigid-hull boat. Also know as the "Zodiac." Brandy grabs Robert's arm and points out the two Zodiac heading towards the Big Island and past their boat. In the Zodiac's were Navy Seals in black wet suits wearing full face mask with tanks.

"God, Robert they look like some space aliens or something, why weren't we told about this action. I told you we shouldn't have reported seeing those Mermaids…." Robert interrupts Brandy.

"We don't really know what is going on. Lets go and talk with Dr. Wilson." Robert said.

As Brandy looks at the two Zodiac's head towards the Big Island on the path of the Mermaids Brandy is just staring in disbelief. She is feeling used, lied too and betrayed by her boss. She looks up at Robert and he said.

"We don't know what is going on and lets not jump to conclusions until we talk with Dr. Wilson." Robert tells Brandy.

"Alright, but he better have a real good reason for not telling us what is going on and why we weren't part of the discussion to send in the Seals."

Inside the ship Brandy and Robert soon find Dr. Wilson in the map room which is also used as a conference room. Dr. Wilson and several other staffers are listing to conversations between the Seals and there surface support team on the Navy ship. As Brandy and Robert enter the room Dr. Wilson motions for them to take a seat and listen to the Seals on their radio transmissions.

"We have located what appears to be the end of the lava tube and might be a hiding place for our targets." One of the Seals tells his support team. Brandy looks at Robert then Dr. Wilson.

"What is going on Dr. Wilson I thought….." She interrupted by Dr. Wilson.

"Brandy, Robert we will fill you two in what has taken place after they finish this mission." Dr. Wilson concludes.

"We are entering the tube with camera on and light." One of the Seals relies to the Surface support team.

Within a couple minutes the Seals Surface Support Team is calling for the Seal Team.

"Team six your location." The Support Team ask.

No one responds and silence on the radio for a few seconds then.

"Service Support Team, Seal Team Six we……" The remainder of the message is garbled, no one can understand what he was saying.

Dr. Wilson looks around the room. Brandy and Robert look at him and the others in the room. Jing finally shows up. The Support Team continues to attempt to contact Seal Team Six.

Brandy walks up to Dr. Wilson and ask.

"What is going on Dr. Wilson." He raises his hands and motions for her to be quit. Robert and I don't have a clue what is going on Jing."

"I did not have time to talk with you both, but even after you informed me of the sighting, the Navy already had them on radar and the Seals were in pursuit."

Dr. Wilson said.

"I thought we all agreed to pursue these Mermaids together and then make a decision of what would be our policy and practice in dealing with these Mermaids in the future." Robert said.

"That was our plan but the Navy wanted to make sure it would be safe for all of us before

we got into the water with these so called Mermaids." Dr. Wilson said.

"Maybe that wasn't such a bad idea since we haven't even heard from the Seal Team."

Brandy tells them.

Just then the radio comes alive with a member of Seal Team Six. The team member voice is clear but he was under stress and the voice was loud as one was very excited.

"We have made contact encountered ambush in the tube by the males. Two seals injured Mermaids 2 Seals 0 we are returning to the ship."

"We don't know what happened in that lava tube so please keep us informed Dr. Wilson, so we can develop our own plans with these Mermaids and Mermen." Robert ask.

"I will, we don't know what happened inside that tube.

We just don't know what happened but I will find out for us and let you guys know as soon as I hear anything." Dr. Wilson concludes.

Brandy and Robert return to the aft deck using there binoculars to see if they can ascertain what has happened to the Navy Seals. As they both look at the two Seal Teams head towards there ship they can see some of the members adding one member in each Zodiac, In the mean time Brandy, Jing and Robert return to their quarters waiting for Dr. Wilson to call them. Brandy is playing with Ariel on the bed and Robert is talking to Fat Cat next to the window. Just then Robert hears a pounding noise coming from the bottom area of the boat and right under his window. Robert still holding Fat Cat looks over at Brandy and Jing perplexed look.

"What is going on, who is making that banging noise?" Jing ask.

"No, listen it is coming from under the boat right under our window." Robert replies.

Jing puts Ariel down but can't see anything and walks port hole to look over the side of the boat but can not see anything. The banging continues. Robert motions to Brandy without saying a word to follow him up the stairs to the deck where they can see over the railing into the ocean and try and figure out what is making that noise. Robert, Jing and Brandy are standing at the railing now looking over the side into the water.

"Are you seeing what I am seeing?" Robert said to Jing and Brandy.

"Yes, O my God, it is a real Mermaid, is it real Robert?" She ask.

"What do you think Jing, are they friendly?" Robert ask.

"Yes, She is motioning for us to follow her, look there are males with her, she is even a little scary looking but why us and how do they know who we are, I mean." Robert concludes.

"They know they can trust us, they just know, like Axum Razor, your first impression or gut instinct is always the right one and they know they can trust us. So what do we do. Follow them underwater or do we report this incident again and risk their lives again or do we discover these Mermaids then figure out how to protect them." Brandy said. "Lets suit up then sneak off this boat and follow the Mermaids. Lets find out what they want from us." Robert tells Brandy and Jing.

"I hope they don't want to eat us." Brandy and Jing laugh.

Brandy looks over the side once again as the Mermaids tread water next to their cabin window. Without exchanging a word Brandy and Jing looks at the Mermaids. They know they will soon be in the water with them. The Mermaids also know that all three of them will be swimming away with them into the unknown. The Mermen smile to ease any tensions.

Brandy, Jing and Robert suited up in their cabin and go below to get tanks for their journey with the Mermaids. As they open the hatch on the side of the ship a light goes on the bridge. The Seamen reports the light to the Captain. The Captain is talking to Dr. Wilson and tells the Seaman.

"Go down below and check it out. Let me know." The Captain orders.

The Seamen walks down the stairs to the diving deck

below. As he walks into the deck area he see's Brandy, Jing and Robert step off the diving deck into the ocean. He also see's a pod of Mermaids waiting for them as they all dive into the abyss. The Seamen struggles to get his radio out of his pocket and calls the bridge.

"Bridge this is Seamen Collins, Doctor Walters, all three of them just jumped off the diving deck into the water with the Mermaids."

"What should I do?" He ask.

"Leave the diving deck down and return to the bridge copy." The Captain orders.

On the bridge Dr. Wilson orders the Captain to maintain this position. Dr. Wilson orders the Captain to maintain silence about the incident for all the staff on the bridge

Dr. Wilson knows that all three are wearing full face mask and can talk with him. That they will not be in deep water because the Mermaids have to come to the surface every twenty to twenty five minutes to get air. Dr. Wilson walks down the hallway from the bridge into the radio room. He also instructs the young radioman to keep silence about any communications he has with doctors Walters. Dr. Wilson sits down at the radio table and dials in to Robert and Brandy.

"This is Dr. Wilson calling the Walters over." He ask.

"This is Robert, sorry we had to take off so soon over." Robert answers.

"How are those Sea BOB F7 working out for you guys." Dr. Wilson ask.

"We have three Mermaids hanging on for a free ride, over" Robert said.

"You know you guys are ridding on the worlds fastest under water sleds." Dr. Wilson tells them.

"We know Dr. Wilson."" We are following a small pod of Mermaids towards a cave below La Pahoa Hoe on the Big island, might be where these Mermaids live. Some type of hand sginles pointing towards the Hammer head shark. Our Navy Seals attack the shark with a stund gun. The shark swims away. They know and swim back into the cave. They are trying to commutate to us. We are about to enter the cave and might not be able to talk with you for a little while, please do not send the Calvary we are ok Dr. Wilson." Robert said. "We will contact you ASAP over." Brandy tells Dr. Wilson. Soon the Merman are also positiong themselves into the cave area.

Dr. Wilson post divers every ten feet to call out for help if needed for all communications. Wilson. The Navy Seals all look towards the Commander for instructions and he gives the ok to return to the Mermaids.

"Alright we have had two of our own injured from these creatures and I do not want anyone else injured. I want all of you on our Sea Bob F7 with weapons just in case we need them. This time I will be onboard with you and we are not going to engage these creatures unless fired upon. We are only going to the entrance and wait for the doctors to return to the entrance and we will escort them back to their ship. Do I make my self clear gentlemen. The Commander ask.

"Yes Sir." The Navy Seals answer.

Soon seven Sea Bob's F7 leave the driving area of the Navy ship heading towards the entrance of the Mermaids. Each navy Seal has his own Sea Bob F7 fully loaded with weapons. Again they are dressed in full black diving gear with full facemask. They soon arrive near the entrance of the tube and position themselves in the boulders outside the entrance.

As Brandy and Robert enter the cave on their Sea Bob F7 with Mermaids swim alongside them. Their are male Mermaids, half fish and human swimming on the sides of the cave standing guard with spears much like one' that have been found in sharks all over the world and most likely the Navy Seals when they entered the cave without permission. The cave is round much like a lava tube, maybe from Mona Kaia many thousand years ago. The cave is shallow and is only about fifty feet under the water. The light from the surface enters and lights up the cave as they head towards the surface. The cave is about thirty meters around and has area's that have been dug out to sit or sleep in. This is where Brandy, Jing and Robert parked the Sea Bobs.

Brandy ask Jing and Robert if these Mermaids sleep in these dugouts how do they breathe if they have to get air every twenty to twenty five minutes. Without even looking at the Mermaids escorting them making no sounds hand signals only to Brandy as she enters the cave. "We use the dugout for protection in case a shark that might enter our cave. Also to protect us from your soldiers like this morning, We sleep on the surface like your kind but hidden away from your kind. We are the old humans.

While processing what Brandy, Jing and Robert both just heard from one of the Mermaids they all surface from under the water and at a quick look around they are now in the middle of lava rocks in the ocean away from humans. Brandy, Jing and Robert still wearing full face mask turn around and for the first time up close look at what they have been calling Mermaids. The face resembles a humans and that is it. They look just like on that special Brandy starts to tell Robert then watches the Mermaids using some type of signing to us." Brandy can't help but fell and little afraid of them as their teeth are razor sharp and pointed for tearing into fish. They have hair but it was very straight. From the waist up they are human and the other half is all fish.

Brandy, Jing and Robert don't dare to take off their full mask as it is too hard to put back on without help and neither of them are that comfortable with these Mermaids and Mermen they are thinking.

"The old looking Mermaid using her hand signals somehow picks up on questions and some answers regarding breathing every twenty or so minutes. They demonstrate how two or three will visit the surface.

"We do not want to harm anyone. You three are good humans. Your Shark people want to harm us." The female Mermaids points to the others with her long fingernails as her fish tail moves back and forth in the water as it lights up.

Brandy can't help admire that tail with all that force in the water and how it lights up as if someone had a light switch to turn on the light in her tail.

The older Mermaid puts her hands on Brandy and Jings shoulders looks them in the eyes and smiles showing her teeth. Just then a ten foot hammer head shark swims buy, the Mermaids and Merman, react by signaling others of the danger,

Brandy watches the Mermaids make growling noise and using their hands to alert others of the weapons of the Navy Seals trying to explain the under water guns and the Sea Bob.

Brandy looks over at Robert and nods to leave and return back to the ship but she wants to get some answers from these Mermaids before she returns to Dr. Wilson and all the beaurcates questions. Robert looks at her and knods his head.

Brandy and the scientist document every hand and movement of the Mermaids to better understand them. Brandy told everyone she was able to communicate with the old Mermade not having to speak a word she said.

We will do everything within our power to keep our people away from your people. Not all our people are bad people. Can we meet with you again?" Brandy ask.

"Yes next time I want to talk with your child Jing." "Your mate was good not to talk in front of our mates after that last incident with your dark men as they would have viewed that as disrespectful." The old one said.

"We have been following you and your family for a long time even when you ride boards in waves. We have listen to you in the surf. This is why we have chosen you humans to help us. We will not survive without your help. We can kill the sharks that try and eat us but we cannot fight your people sharks who shoot spears at us, who send noises in our water that kill us and our friends." I will send my people to you when we can meet again." The Mermaid concludes.

The pod of male and female Mermaids tread the water listing in their minds of what Brandy and the old Mermaids concludes.

"How long have you and your kind lived in the ocean?" Brandy ask.

Many, Many moons young one." The old Mermaid answers.

"Did you live on land like us at one time?" Brandy ask., until the land exploded with black rock, we started to live in the water and eat here.

We even looked like you." She said.

Brandy and Robert look around and see all the Mermaids laughing.

"We need you and your partner to keep shark people away from killing our people. You two are kind and may not be able to stop all the shark people but maybe you can let us know when shark people are coming after us." She tells Brandy.

"We will, we will." Brandy assures her.

Brandy tells her.

"We must return to the ship for air." as she points at her tanks.

The old Mermaid nods her head and goes into the water. Brandy, Jing and Robert follow her. Soon they are on their water sleds heading towards the entrance again escorted by the Merman. Robert looks over and watches the males swimming so fast and the other hanging onto the sled for a free ride, they look at Robert and smile.

As Robert see's the entrance to the cave he can see other Sea Bob sleds off in the distance with Navy Seals sitting on the sleds. Robert immediately motions to the male Mermen to get off the sled and tells them telepathy to return back into the cave there are shark people waiting for them. Immediately they break off and swim back into the cave.

Brandy and Jing sitting behind Robert said "Good buy." to the Mermen.

"Dr. Wilson we are now leaving the cave and returning to the ship escorted by Navy

Seals." Brandy said.

Brandy, Jing and Robert look to make sure they are being followed by the Seal Team and they are not taking retaliatory measures against the Mermaids. They all were following them to the ship.

Soon they are all at the ship. They park there sleds next to one another and take off all their gear in the drive room. The Commander of the Seal Team tells his men.

"Go ahead and take off your gear and go eat and rest while I meet with the good doctors in the briefing room."

Brandy, Jing and Robert leave the dive room together without saying a word to anyone. Both of them are feeling mixed emotions about the Mermaids and the Navy Seal members injured by the Mermaids. On one hand Brandy, Jing or Robert do not like anyone getting hurt.especially our own Navy Seals. As a rule scientist are caring people and are committed to protecting all species. In the ocean they feel protective for all that inhabits and now they feel akin to the Mermaids because of our experience of communicating with them.

Inside the conference room the Navy Commander followed Brandy, Jing and Robert 47.from the dive room. Now in the conference room Dr. Wilson, two other males from the State Department, two females from the CIA.

Dr. Wilson introduces all the parties and starts off the meeting by discussing why these people are here.

"As you all know Doctors Brandy, Jing and Dr. Robert just had an encounter with actual Mermaids and frankly I can't wait to hear what transpired between them?" Dr. Wilson said.

"We will be happy to inform all of you as soon as we

know who you are and what you are doing here." Brandy ask as she turns to Dr. Wilson.

"Oh I am sorry Brandy, this is Tom Haden and Ken Perkins from the State Department and Monica and Carrie from the CIA Langue school. They are here to help the CIA with their vast resoures in langues and can help all of you with telepathic communications." The State Department to assist us with other countries and White House interest. Dr. Wilson concludes.

"Starting with Tom tell Doctors Waters why you two are here please." Dr. Wilson ask.

Tom from the State Department smiles and turns to Brandy, Jing and Robert and said.

"You know we have been on board the ship and we are only concerned how this information is protected and shared with other countries. He concludes.

"Ok Monica, your turn." Doctor Wilson said.

"We came on board with the State Department personnel. Our only interest is how do these Mermaids communicate. We head up the CIA langue school and we find these findings a break through for us and our countries defense. She concludes.

"I don't know about that, but Robert and I and our daughter Jing find this information on how the Mermaids communicate is a wonderful development. But more important right now is what we plan to do to meet their request that we protect them from what they describe as Shark people meaning us, human people. Let me start from the beginning.

The old Mermaids reported to me that our Shark people the Navy Seal Team attacked them with spears…." Brandy is interrupted by the Navy Seal Commander. "That is nuts, they attacked us without cause and…" The Commander is stopped by Dr. Wilson.

"Please Commander", ask Dr.Waters, "This is a debriefing on the conversation she had with the Mermaids. This is not an investigation or inquiry by NCIS for a court marshall or procusation Commander."

"Go ahead Brandy." Dr. Wilson said.

"Ok, The old Mermaid described all humans who attack them as Sharks are there only enemy in the ocean. They are asking us to protect them from all sharks or they won't survive. I really don't understand why they have chosen me, Robert and Jing to help them." Brandy paused for a minute the Navy Commandeer speaks up.

"Why should we protect them. You should see what they did to my Seal, he….Dr. Wilson interrupts him again and said.

"That is enough Commander. This meeting is over, I will contact all you for the next meeting. I apologize Brandy for the outburst from the Navy Commander." Dr. Wilson concludes.

Dr. Wilson looks around the room and the other department heads are shaking their heads in disbelief of the Commanders behavior.

Brandy and Robert return to their quarters. Inside they look at each other and shake there heads in disbelief of what just occurred. Brandy tells Robert and Jing.

"You know I can understand why the Commander is upset about his Seals being hurt but has to look at what we are doing is history and has all types of applications for humanity, from doctors in surgery talking to doctors and nurses through telepathy not distracting anyone to listing to what our enemies are thinking. Brandy concludes.

"Let have a beer honey and a diet Pepsi for our little one." Robert suggest to Brandy.

"Sounds great babe." Brandy said.

About a half hour later Dr. Wilson calls their quarters and ask them to meet him in the conference room. Inside the conference room everyone is there except the Navy Commander,

"Ok as you can see the Navy Commander will not be here. The Secretary of the Navy has assured me that the Seals will not be dispatched on any of our cruses. That have been ordered back to Pearl. Now that we have that taken care of that problem Robert, Jing and Brandy please continue debriefing us on the Mermaids."

Robert and I were looking over the side of portside of the ship when we saw the Mermaids looking up at us. They motioned for us to come with them and as you know we did. As we road on our Sea Bob F7 male Mermaids grabbed on and road with us. It was real fun and a little scary as these are the guys that just injured our Navy Seals. But I felt safe, I did not realize at that point they could read my mind or thoughts." Brandy said.

"Actually a calming feeling came over me when they grabbed on to the sea scooter. It was a good feeling. It was only a little scary when we entered the cave or lava hole and we saw all those male Mermen with weapons." Robert concluded.

Jing speaks up. "It was fun, I had these huge Merman on each side of my Sea Bob hanging on as we went through the ocean into their cave." The women in the room smile.

Brandy continues debriefing the group. After telling them the details Dr. Wilson opens the debriefing up to questions from its members. The first questions comes from Monica.

"So tell me at what point did you know that they were communicating with you without talking aloud Brandy or Robert please." She ask.

Brandy speaks up. "I realized the old Mermaid was communicating with me when I could answer her without saying a verbal word. She would respond to my questions. I think I can let you feel a little of what I was feeling. Monica and the rest of you look into the persons eyes next to you. Don't look at anything else. Let your brain relax and send words to them, just a few words using the eyes as a gateway to their brain.. now ask the person next to you to tell you what you said. Wait for a second for them to communicate to you. It is something like that, starting with you Monica what did Carrie tell you." Brandy ask.

"That she wanted to go and see the Mermaids in person." Carrie turns and looks at Monica in disbelief.

"I can't believe you just said that, that is exactly what message I was sending to you." She clapped her hands and smiled. Monica speaks up. "So please continue Brandy." She tells them." "I have written down the questions and answers she gave me. I have a copy for each of you. If you have questions about the Q and A just ask us.

Tom from the State Department ask Robert. "Robert at any time did these sea creatures communicate with you directly."

Excuse me Tom, lets all use the same names describing

these half humans half fish by calling them Mermaids or Mermen ok." Dr. Walters ask.

"No, I was able to listen to the conversation between Brandy and the Old Mermaid." Robert answers. "Ok, were you able to listen from the initial conversation or at what point did you start hearing there conversation in your mind." Tom ask.

"I think I heard everything the old women was telling Brandy. I have read Brandies notes and I think I heard all those questions and the answers from the old women." Robert answers.

Jing speaks up. "She refereed to themselves as the Old people, she had gray hair, long finger nails and just looked old."

"Ok, Next Dr. Wilson ask.

"Yes, either of you tell us what they want, I don't quite understand what they expect us to do to protect them from shark people meaning us or humans in the water." Tom ask from the State Department.

"I asked that question to the old one and she only said if we do not help them they will die.

For example there people are dying because the Navy is testing with low frequency waves underwater since 2006 as I have been informed and it is killing their people. Also their are ships dragging nets all over the place and…She stopped as he holds his hands up "I have heard enough. I don't mean to be rude, but the old women did not tell you all those things did she." Ken ask.

"She told me that and more, that the Navy is killing their people with the sound wave in the water, killing dolphins, whales, all their friends in other words all the mammals in the ocean. Let's not try and walk around this issue it is well known both of your agencies are in bed with this testing all over the world. Including all agencies that deal with the ocean and defense.

The bottom line here is that we either stop doing things in the oceans that kill off this species along with all the other mammals to use against our enemies or we preserve and protect this species for generations in the future. These people are part human and I believe they were all human and walked on land at one time. They reported to Brandy they walked on land before the lands erupted. The Mermaids reported exactly what 51. Dr.Mathews reported and believes that all of us came from the oceans. Just considering this hypotheses and some research they can provide knowledge to our society that no one on earth can provide and that is telepathic communications. In turn we should provide protection at all cost for this population of part human and fish for all man kind."

Brandy concludes. They also can scream in the water to each other just another method of communications to get the attention of others. I think this explains the history of sierons noise from Mermaids. Brandy concludes.

There is complete silence in the room. Everyone is thinking and absorbing what Brandy has told them, they are writing notes realizing this has become so important not only for our country but for our world.

Dr. Wilson speaks up. "This discovery is far reaching and so very important that we need to inform the White House. I will get their backing before we do anything further.

I will let all of you know what is happening as soon

as I hear anything. Now Jing, Brandy and Robert do not leave this ship until I get clearances to do so. We have protocols in place that we all agreed on and for your security. Understood. If the Mermaids return and ask you doctors to follow them tell them you can't right now but will come to them very soon. Of course you let me know right away if they have made contact with you. Alright that is it for the time being.

Brandy, Jing and Robert walk back to their cabin and sit on the couch with Fat Cat and. Brandy's dog Ariel.

"So what do you think is going to happen now." Jing ask.

"I think this whole thing is going to the President like Dr. Wilson said and I think our President Mrs. Clinton will order the Navy and there projects that are killing the Mermaids and Merman to stop." Brandy said.

"I think you may be right darling. Clinton has been a real supporter of NOAA and protecting our ocean and the things in it. Robert responded.

"What role do you think the Navy will play in this support for the Mermaids" Brandy ask.

"I don't think they will play any role in their future, they let the Mermaid's die after they killed her relatives with soniar testing. They can't restrain themselves around these Mermaids we have seen this morning and they only have one goal in mind and that is conquering everything in the ocean. They can not be stewards of the Mermaids or any other mammals as they are responsible for killing hundred if not thousands of creatures in the ocean with their testing. Robert concludes.

As there conversation ended the cabin phone rings. It is

Dr. Wilson and he wants to see all of them in the conference room right away.

Inside the conference room is Dr. Wilson only. He is smiling and said.

"Ok you doctors, sit down we have some good news. First I want all of you to know that the Administration is behind us completely, Homeland Security, and the White House.

Our own security personnel and the Homeland people will be with us through the mission. Our mission is now is to locate, count these Mermaids and Mermen so we can develop a plan to protect them from all humans. Now your specific mission is to learn how these people communicate with each other. Our National security depends on your ability to learn how they do this." Dr. Wilson concludes.

"When can we start." ask Robert.

"As soon as we can check the weather, let the other department heads know we are moving forward. Also you doctors can meet with our own security to back you guys up. I want to use our own people first ok. "Dr. Wilson said.

"Alright we will do that and when we are ready to dive I will notify you doctor." Brandy said.

Brandy and Robert meet with their agency's security chief and discuss what type of backup they are looking for and what their personnel may encounter. They discuss what happened to the Navy Seals and why it happened. Robert makes a point that he does not want them right outside the entrance to the cave. Just a little distance away where they will not be any threat to the Mermaids.

Inside Brandy and Roberts cabin Brandy hugs Ariel and Robert hugs fat Cat. They look at each other, now realizing that this mission could be very dangerous and also very rewarding. A lot of people are waiting for the results and answers to questions about telepathic communications that is millions of years old. Brandy smiles at Robert and he hugs her just for a minute. Not saying a word communicating their love for each other without saying a word. Brandy looks at Robert and wonders if this could be the answer on how to communicate telepathically. Jing looks at both of them and said. "What about me." Brandy speaks up and said. "Come here baby we love you too.

After a short rest in their cabin Robert receives a call from Dr. Wilson who request they dive one more time today. He said. "The White House would like a call later today to report our progress."

"Soon they are in the drive tank suiting up with staff to go down and meet with the Mermaids and Mermen. Brandy takes a minute and calls Dr. Wilson.

"Hi Doctor we are almost ready to drive again. We have divers from Homeland and our own Security staff to back us up. I really don't know if they will talk to us but we are going to try. The tide is high tonight and I think the weather will hold for now." Brandy concludes.

"I think you are right Brandy. Be careful and don't take any chances. We can take this slow if you guys decide. Is Jing diving with you?" Dr. Wilson explains.

"Yes she is doctor. Thank you doctor." Brandy answers.

"Just keep an eye out for her." The doctor ask.

All the divers are now suited up and are on their Sea Bob F7 sea subs and take off for the Mermaids cave. Within ten minutes they are at the cave entrance. Only Brandy, Jing and Robert approach the entrance. They enter about ten feet when they are meet by the Merman with spears and other weapons. This time all the Mermen were friendly and again grabbed onto the sea subs and road into the inter center of the pod. Sitting on a set of Hugh rocks sat the old one. Brandy thought and said to her without uttering a verbal word.

"We are back with good news."

The Mermaid responded as she swam over to Brandy. The old one put her arms on Brandy's shoulders and her long fingernails clenched onto Brandy's wetsuit. Brandy wanted to scream but keep her composure. Brandy dismisses any negative thoughts and forces herself to think only positive thoughts and she is only inches away from the face of this person who looks like some monster from the deep but Brandy knows she is human and part fish. Brandy tells her.

"I need you to tech me how you communicate with each other and me. I need to learn this so I can teach others so we can all communicate all over the waters." Brandy answers her telepathic.

"The old one nods her head and has Brandy follow her onto the rock. Jing is doing her own telepathic communications with the younger girls. Robert is hanging with the Mermen watching Brandy and the old one communicate. The old one motions to Brandy to remove her diving mask. Brandy looks at Robert and he gives the nod, feeling it is safe for Brandy to do so. Robert swims up behind Brandy and helps her remove the mask and turns off the tank to save O2. Brandy is now looking at the Mermaids face to face and about one foot apart. As Brandy looks at her she realizes that this lady once lived on the earth just like her until the volcanoes exploded all over the world and forced everyone into the waters. That this Mermaid was once as beautiful as any women on earth. But in order to survive they moved into the oceans. Brandy looks into the Mermaids eyes and finds a kind and genital women who's only wish is to be with her family and be safe away from mankind, us humans also known as sharks their worst enemies. Brandy tells her through ESP or her thoughts that "Our people have agreed to protect all of you in the waters that we control with no noise from our ships and no more noise or low frequency testing in the waters. Our people want to learn how to communicate, talk using thought only and no words." Brandy told the old Mermaid.

"No one taught me but I think we just learned how to communicate under water by our actions which could translate into words and at some time we were able to send thoughts to each other. I am looking at you right now in your eyes. You understand me, if I turn my head you can not hear my thoughts. Also if I scream under water I will get your attention" The Mermaid said. "Ok, so if we practice looking at each other and communicate with our minds and eyes we will at some point be able to communicate with each other right." Brandy ask.

"We all know what to do and when to do it, for example when a real shark comes close to our people we all know to grab weapons and attack the shark from eating us. No words need to be said, but if we need to communicate we can make sounds in the water that travel through the water waves, like our friends the whales, dauphins and other warm blood friends all communicate through the waves of the water. Your shark people send communications through the water that kill our people and all our friends." The old Mermaid said with a sad face.

"I know it will not happen again. We made a mistake and now will protect all people of the water." Brandy replies.

The old Mermaid looks Brandy in the eyes up close and smiles and shows her sharp teeth as a jester of acceptance to Brandy.

Brandy tell the Mermaid. "I will now seek out other water people…Brandy is interrupted by the Mermaid.

"You must wear this shell necklace to show all the other water people you are one of us and not a shark person. When you see another water person show them this necklace and they will communicate with you. If you are hungry they will feed you. If you need to sleep that will protect you. Always be honest when communicating and always be our friend and we will always be your friend." The old Mermaid concludes.

"I have a couple more questions. Where should we go to let other water people know we will protect them and they can come to us for help when they need help." Brandy ask.

"We will send messengers to the others. They live in the caves of the Volcanoes throughout the waters. Then they will send messengers and soon all people of the water know. The mermaid replies.

"If any of your people need help at any time they can contact us by contacting the ships with NOAA or our Coast Guard ship with the red stripe. All our people will be alerted and will help all water people when they ask us and they will let me know also. You can also contact me this way or…. Brandy is interrupted by the old Mermaid.

"Brandy we have seen you, your daughter Jing and

Robert many times in the waves. We have watched all of you have fun on boards. We have listened to you many times and we decided to contact you two for help." The old Mermaid said.

"So you know where we live, that is so cool, I love it. So if you need help I will see you when we are surfing in front of our house." Brandy smiles. Brandy looks over at Robert and Jing without saying a word she tells him it is time to go and she needs help putting on her full mask. Robert responds with out saying a word.

Soon Brandy's mask is on and she say's goodbye to the old one and dives into the cave with Robert and Jing in tow. As all three of them ride on there Sea Bob water sled they are again accompanied by Mermen on each side smiling and having fun on the ride.

They break off when they see other men on water sleds, there escorts to the ship.

Upon approach to the NOAA ship Brandy, Jing and Robert see another ship anchored next to their ship. Soon inside the drive room Brandy, Jing and Robert take off their gear and go to meet with Dr.Wilson. Inside the conference room to their surprise is full of NOAA personnel, CIA and Homeland staff sitting next to Dr. Wilson is a delegation of Japanese personnel. Sitting with them is Dr. Tanaka and she is not smiling.

"Alright everyone please, may I have your attention. Thank you, we can now get this meeting underway. Dr. Wilson ask. Looking around the room for compliance from the guest aboard the ship.

Soon it is all quit, one could hear a pin drop or the water from Brandies hair which was still wet and water dripping onto the chair beside her. Brandy takes her towel and removes the water.

"All of you are here about Doctors Brandy, Jing and Roberts meeting with the Mermaids and how they communicate with each other. Also the Japanese have filed a protest with our State Department because they reported that they made first contact or at lease saw these Mermaids first and we just took advantage of their reporting. I am acknowledging that the Japanese counter part to our NOAA first spotted the Mermaids at this location and we simply took there reporting and made contact in United States waters without there assistance. Since we do not need permission to do research in our waters we consider the matter closed unless the Japanese would like to protest further." Dr. Wilson concludes.

No one from the Japanese delegation comments. Dr. Wilson address Jing, Robert and Brandy.

"As you doctors know this is a very important meeting for many agencies and for history as we know it. We recorded and made a movie of this historic meeting today and I want all of you to share in it. The knowledge that we all take from this historical meeting will for ever change how we communicate." Dr. Wilson concluded.

Dr. Wilson turns on the movie and he turns and looks at all in the room. They are fascinated with the recorded meeting with the Mermaids and Mermen. As the recording ends Dr. Wilson turns on the lights and said.

"All of you know what we know but as I caution all of you to keep what you have witnessed today secret from all our people. As you know we in the free world have many enemies and for us to develop this superior manor of communicating with each other we must not let our enemies obtain this information. Some of our enemies live among us so please protect this information." He concludes.

"I would like to address the Japanese doctors here with us and get some feedback of where they think we should start with this data now." Dr. Wilson ask.

Dr. Hanaka speaks up. "On behalf of our country and our research team I want to thank you for inviting us here today. Our Leaders have agreed to protect this information we learned today in the most secret way from the population. Our research team suggest we continue the search for more pods as we first suggested. That we start our search in the island of Aogashima two hundred twenty two miles in the Philippine Ocean. Both Mermaids and Mermen have been spotted by Pearl divers from the Philippine semen and divers. The only draw back to this location is that sneaker waves as high as one hundred feet have been seen coming into this island so we need to be very careful with our staff equipment and diving teams." She said.

"Ok, Aogashima Island it is. All the rest of you folks from the State Department, CIA Language School doctors, Homeland Security and Japanese Research Team doctors can use this conference room to set up your studies. Also we have now the U.S. Coast Guard with our team. Doctors Brandy, Jing and Robert Walters are available to all of you at any time. The cameras and recording equipment in this room is running and we have security men here to protect that equipment and also all of you. They have assured me they will stay out of your way and not interfere with any of your request or testing. Good luck now." Dr. Wilson concludes and walks out of the room.

Brandy and Jing enter their cabin and walk over to the bed and just flop down on the bed. Ariel, Brandy's dog and Fat cat both jump on the bed with both of them. Fat cat is purring and Ariel is kissing Brandy. Robert heads to the shower.

"Can you believe what we just did Robert?" Brandy shouts out.

"No I can't believe what happened, it is like someone special in our lives that has brought all of us together. I need a beer how about you darling." Robert yells back.

"I need more than one beer. I agree something or someone very special has chosen us to help the Mermaids. I am having a little bit of hard time getting my head around this whole event, but I am enjoying every minute of this babe." Brandy concludes.

After a couple hours the telephone rings in Brandy and Roberts cabin. It is Dr. Wilson he is requesting they meet him on the deck. They all meet on the deck.

"The reason I asked you two to meet me here is that we are out of rooms to have a meeting place I think we need a bigger boat. Anyway what do you guys think about going to this island Aogashima. The Coast Guard advised me that it is a very dangerous island to anchor off. The reason it is that they have these sneaker waves as high as a one hundred feet high. They can capsize a ship. Despite popular mythology that has sprung up about the predictability of waves it is not true that every seventh wave is a big one. These sneaker waves occur when two large waves converge and suddenly create a monster wave as the wind drive this wave onto the beaches far up from the foam of a normal wave. Victims of these waves have reported that the wave grabs you as you try to run up the beach and drags you into the water." All I am saying we need to think about our next chose of islands." Dr. Wilson concludes. "lets go ahead to the Japanese island. This will keep them involved in the process and through the risk could be very dangerous we need make contact with that pod of Mermaids."

"In fact with all Mermaids everywhere in the oceans regardless of the risk. After all we are the ones who have killed many of them from our testing of low frequency Sonair transmission." Dr. Wilson said.

"You doctors need to go and meet with all those doctors in the conference room. They want to pick your brains about how you two communicated with the Mermaids." Dr. Wilson said and he smiles and walks off to the bridge.

Inside the conference room Brandy, Jing and Robert meet with all the doctors on this project. One of the doctors starts by saying.

"Thank you for meeting with so soon after your meeting with the Mermaids. We think that your recall will be more clear and you will be able to assist us in understanding this new technology to interact with the Mermaids." Oh I am sorry I fore got to introduce myself and the other doctors. I am Doctor Leone, this is Doctor Percher, Doctor Davis and Doctor Walden. We are researchers and professors at various Universities all with the same goals of trying to understand this new technology. We have reviewed your tapes of your meeting with the old Mermaid. Each of us now have questions because as you can see there is no audio on the tape. We need to know what was said and when and what you experienced then each of us have a set of questions to ask each of you ok." She concludes.

For the next hour Brandy, Jing and Robert answer the doctors questions and demonstrate how the ESP works in terms of communication with the Mermaids. Doctor Walden ask Brandy.

"Brandy, at what point did you realize she was sending or asking you a question in your brain."

"I think I knew right away, I mean the question was or her message came inside my brain as if she had said it to me verbally. You just know she is sending you a message or telling you something because she is looking you right in the eyes. The questions or statements are real clear and to the point." Brandy concludes.

"You said earlier Brandy that the old Mermaid said she knew where you Jing and Robert lived on Oahu because she watched all of you surf. Do you think she might have been educating both of you to their way of communicating long before you two met." Doctor Davis ask.

"That is a great question, I just don't know what the answer is doctor, but if you discover it please share it with us." Brandy said.

the meeting is concluded with more questions than answers. As Brandy, Jing and Robert walk to their quarters Robert tells Brandy.

"At lease we are helping the Mermaids. Not destroying them like the Navy was." he concludes.

"Right, but do you really trust the Navy to step aside. I don't trust them and we need to work with our security people to make sure we have the Intel to keep all of us safe. I heard that a lot of money was put into that low frequency equipment and you know what has happened in the past with our military people not following orders." Brandy tells Jing and Robert.

Jing walks over to the stern and looks at the Japanese ship leading the way. Jing tells them a story.

"According to Japanese folklore entire pod of Mermaids live all around the island. When fishermen are returning from fishing and before they dock they must throw two fish over board for the Mermaids. If for some reason they forget or refuse to the Mermaids will sink there ship and kill one deckhand." Robert laughs and replies.

"Thank God we are not fishermen in that village." Robert said.

"I don't think it would be that bad unless you were one of the fishermen that refused to help feed the Mermaids." Brandy replied.

"Very true how about some dinner and then we will walk Ariel and Fat Cat." Robert ask.

"I am starving lets eat." Brandy replied.

As they walked away from the stern of the ship Brandy notices a ship way off in the horizons. For a minute she thinks it might be that Navy ship but dismisses the idea.

Soon they are eating shrimp, lobster, in butter with wedges of lemon along with a giant crab legs. Baked potatoes and mixed salad with several types of wines and beers along with French beads.

While Brandy and Robert are eating Dr. Wilson joined them at their table. Brandy ask Dr. Wilson.

"Do you really think the Navy is going to back off this research project like the Secretary of the Navy ordered them to." Brandy ask.

Dr. Wilson looks at Brandy, Jing and Robert with a stern face and said.

"They better or there will be hell to pay I can tell you both. Now lets eat and then get some rest we have a long ways to go ok." Dr. Wilson concludes.

For the next two days Brandy, Jing and Robert conduct research along with other doctors on board. They have meetings and discuss their finding with Dr. Wilson. At one of the meetings Dr. Wilson warns everyone to be carefull on deck because of possible rogue waves. He tells everyone of these monster waves and the largest one ever recorded was one feet. During the meeting one of the doctors ask Dr. Wilson what causes these waves. Dr. Wilson replies.

"These waves also called extreme waves and gravity waves travel at different speeds, so they can pile up and possible capsize a ship like ours, so please be careful on deck."

The next morning at 4am Brandy, Jing and Robert are woken up as they are thrown from there bed onto the floor, neither are injured, the lights are out and both are confused as to what had just happened. Jing is thrown from her bed and then runs into her mothers and dad room for safety. Jing ask.

"What just happened Mom."

"Are you ok Jing." Ask Brandy.

"Yes, I am ok how about you two guys." Jing ask.

As Brandy and Robert gather themselves, Ariel and Fat Cat they are soon interrupted by one of ships staff.

"Are you two Ok." he yells out at the door to the cabin.

"Yes we are ok, what happened." Brandy ask as she opens the cabin door.

"We were hit by a Hugh rogue wave, we are in waters that freighters don't travel in and we never know when one of these waves will hit us broadside. Please stay in your quarters until you hear the all clear. Please don't hang out on the deck. We just don't know when one of these waves are coming folks." The Seamen concludes.

Just then another wave slabs the side of the ship but the wave appears to be much smaller. The Seamen yells.

"Hold on everyone."

The next two days they spend in rough weather with swells up to thirty feet. Many of the seamen and doctors are sea sick. Soon they enter calmer waters and see the Island of Aogashima. As you approach the Island of Aogashima she appears beyond the fog that protects her. Much like the Big Island of the Hawaii islands the vague or vapor from the Volcano leaves a mist in the air. This Vogue will follow the airstreams around the island. Jing, Brandy and Robert look at the Island from the ships railing. Brandy tells Jing and Robert.

"Remember when we went to see the picture Cong and in that movie as the ship clears the fog the camera pans and shows the entire island with waves pounding the shore line. That is the impression I get when I am looking at this island." She said.

"So you think there is a giant Gorilla waiting to take you off somewhere and …. Robert is interrupted by Brandy.

"You are sooooo silly, of course not but you have to say it is spooky to look at right." Brandy concludes.

"Right it is spooky looking, I will give that one." Robert said.

"If King Cong was in the island he would come after Jing with her long blond hair." Robert said.

The decision is made by the Japanese to anchor at the north end of the island because this is close to the inlet dock systems that has been developed by the Japanese and the area where Mermaids have been seen by the fishermen many times.

As Brandy, Jing and Robert walk to the conference room to meet Dr. Wilson they look out through one of the port holes and view what appears to be a Navy ship off in the distance appearing to be a private cruse ship. Inside the conference room Brandy tells Dr. Wilson.

"Dr. Wilson we just looked out the starboard port hole and parked out about a mile is what appears to be a Navy ship. Are we going to have problems with them when we are in the water doctor. Brandy ask.

"No, they are there just to back us up incase you guys get in trouble or need immediate assistance other than our Security Personnel who by the way will be diving with all of you. We have no idea how these Mermaids will respond to you three. Buy the way have you two decided how you want to approach these Mermaids when you come in contact with them." Dr. Wilson ask.

"The old women Mermaid said she would notify all old people we were coming and for my Mom to wear this neckless all the time she comes in contact with Mermaids as they will consider her one of them." Jing tells Dr.Wilson.

I think doctor we need to just get into the water and make runs in the Sea Bob F7 Until we make contact. We need our security personnel to keep out of sight but be available in case we need them during the search incase the Mermaids become hostile at some point." Brandy said.

That is a good idea Brandy. We do not want to spook the Mermaids. Do you think they will come up to you on the Sea Bob like the Mermaids in Hawaii. Dr. Wilson ask.

"I just don't know Dr., but Robert and Jing are hoping they do. Dr.Hanaka from Japan will be escorting us along with another one of her staff ridding on their Sea Bob. So if you will coordinate it with them we would appreciate that doctor." Brandy ask.

"No problem." Dr. Wilson responds.

Soon Brandy, Jing and Robert are in the water ridding their underwater Sea Bob and meet up with Dr. Hanaka and her assistant. They are all about thirty feet down heading towards the area where Mermaids were last seen. They are passing large numbers of Seals reaching eight feet in length. Some of the seals weighted about eight hundred pounds. The Seals speed up to the Sea Bob and look at Brandy, Jing, Robert and Dr. Hanaka and her assistant. Off in the distance are two ship wrecks. Both appear to be fishing type boats about fourty feet long. Unlike the muddy Atlantic ocean bottom the pacific ocean close to islands have corral and many different type of fish along with jelly fish passing as the currents take them. They are enjoying all the beauty when two Male Mermaids come up from below and grab onto their Sea Bob. As Brandy turns and looks at the Mermaids one tells her telepathy to follow them. They point upward a very large wave is just passing overhead. Off in the distance both Robert and

Brandy are observing their ship leans over to one side

and come back up. Just then a voice comes over the radio to both of them.

"Doctors there was a Hugh earthquake and we were hit by a Hugh wave. Stay where you are now, repeat do not attempt to surface right now it is too dangerous. We will notify you."

The transmission was broken up but abatable. Brandy and Robert look at each other and continue following the Male Mermaids. Brandy looks over at Dr. Hanaka she is smiling being escorted by two more male Mermaids a series of large waves pass over them before they enter a Hugh cave escorted by more male Mermaids. Some of them have weapons in their hands and are very scary looking with their fish like appearance. When they open their mouth they have sharp teeth which gives the appearance of a half fish and half human that has the sharp teeth to tear away fish to eat. Also realizing that they could bite and tear away any of the divers. Inside the cave which goes up towards the ocean light can be seen. Remembering what the radio operator advised them not to surface because of Hugh waves coming towards the island both Robert and Brandy look at each other. Both are reassured buy one of the Male Mermaids when he tells both of them that where they are located at the surface is safe and the waves can't get them. The male Mermaid smiles and shows his teeth. Brandy is thinking how scary he looks and he reads her thoughts.

The male Mermaid tells Brandy.

"I am sorry but the human race went into the ocean to survive and this is what we turned out to look like."

He assures Brandy that they once looked like her.

Brandy tells him

"I am also sorry and just not use to seeing you guys."

The male Mermaid nods his head, smiles and heads to the surface where Brandy, Jing Robert and Dr. Hanaka and her assistant are all meet by a group of female Mermaids sitting on rocks in this inlet away from the waves of the ocean. Though they can hear the roar of the Hugh waves coming into the Island.

Brandy and Robert take off there breathing mask and Dr. Hanaka and her assistant follow the lead. They swim up and next to the older Mermaid surrounded by younger female Mermaids. The older the Mermaid looks very worried and the roar of the incoming waves is so loud everyone is looking around to see if that wave will enter there lagoon. Just then a Hugh wave hit's the island and a wall of water entered the lagoon taking some of the Mermaids up the side of the lagoon into the back and side of the lagoon killing them. The wait of the water shoved the old women, Brandy, Robert, Jing and Dr. Hanaka along with their Sea Bob's being tossed around like little toys just missing Brandy and Robert but hitting Dr. Hanaka assistant a female graduate student. Her body floats away with the wave and ocean turbulence. Brandy, Jing and Robert travel down back into the cave towards the open ocean. As they are tossed though the water they all struggle to put on their mask to get oxygen. Smaller waves follow. After being tossed around they see a ship being tossed pass them onto the Island. It is not their ship but Dr. Hanaka ship from Japan. As Brandy, Jing and Robert surface they can see their ship off into the distance. Both of them start swimming towards the ship.

Realizing that usually a couple of waves follow an earthquake in the ocean they might be over the worst. Just then Dr. Hanaka appears at the surface, she is very shook up. She has lost one of her students, their ship and crew. She does not know if there is any survivors. Brandy points towards her ship and said.

"look guys, they launched a vessel for us. Come over here with us Dr." Brandy calls out.

Soon the small rescue boat is next to them. The doctors board the craft and head for the ship. Dr. Hanaka continues to look around for her student who was taken by a huge wave.

"hurry up and get on board, drop your tanks and get on the ladder." He yells out.

Soon all are aboard the NOAA ship Brandy, Jing and Robert hurry to their quarters to check on their friends Fat Cat and Sleepy Ariel their dog. Yes they were sleeping on the bed just waiting for Brandy, Jing and Robert. Fat Cat meowed and Ariel just rolled over and smiled like all pugs do. Everyone sigh a moment of relief for themselves and for their friends. All the doctors sit in the chairs quietly just taking a minute of silence to gather their thoughts and thanks to God they serviced the experience with the Mermaids and waves.

After a short rest the telephone rings in their cabin and Robert answer it.

"Hello." Robert answered.

"Hang on you guys, we have yet another Hugh wave coming and….." The phone goes

dead. Robert tells Brandy. "Hang on babe, that was the boss and we have another…." Just then another Hugh wave slam's the ship as it lisp to the side and rocks back up.

Brandy holding onto Ariel and Robert holding Jing. Fat Cat has run under the bed.

Robert call the Captain on the deck.

"This is Dr. Walters, is Dr. Wilson there?" he ask.

"He's right her doctor." The Captain answered as he hands the phone to Dr. Wilson.

"Hi doctor, I don't know if anymore of those waves are coming or not but we are heading back to Hawaii as we talk to get out of this debris field and make room for the U.S. Coast Guard and the Navy which are in the area now. We have even spotted dead bodies floating in the water along with ship gear. It is time to leave and return to our dock.

You, Jing and Brandy stay in your cabin. Once we are out of the danger area I will call all of you. We can get something to eat and debrief you guys along with Dr. Hanaka who is now in her quarters. She is pretty upset about her loss. How about you checking on her for me doctor." he ask.

"Sure no problem." Replies Robert.

Robert informs Brandy and Jing of his conversation with Dr. Wilson and starts towards Dr. Hanaka room when Brandy tells him she is coming also. Both walk to her cabin and knock on the door. Dr. Hanaka opens her door. It is apparent she has been crying because of her loss. She invites Brandy and Robert into her cabin which is small. Robert suggest she comes down to their quarters where they can talk and relax. Dr. Hanaka agreed.

Inside Brandy's and Roberts cabin Dr. Hanaka talks about her experience that morning. She does not know what has happened to all her student aboard their research vesle.

She does not know how many members survived that huge wave and the ship wreck.

Brandy tells her.

"Dr. Hanaka, Dr. Wilson will keep you informed as he receives reports from our Navy and Coast Guard regarding your crew and your boat. You are welcome to stay with Robert and me throughout this ordeal. I am just glad nothing happened to you. Yes we all have scratches' and small cuts from all the debris but we are alive and I thank God for that." Brandy concludes.

"Yes Dr. Hanaka said." Robert speaks up. "We are underway now to Hawaii, our work is done here for now doctors. Please have a seat Dr. Hanaka, how about a diet Pepsi diet Aspertei free and Caffeine free."

"Yes, thank you doctor." She answers.

Soon Dr. Wilson calls on the boat phone. Brandy answers. "Hello."

"This is Dr. Wilson and I need you doctors and Dr. Hanaka in the conference room. It's not good news for Dr. Hanaka. Our Coast Guard and Navy ship have recovered her ships crew and the students onboard the ship. I want to be the one to inform her. See you in five minutes." Dr. Wilson hangs up.

Inside the conference room Dr. Wilson along with the Navy commander, Cost Guard commander and Captain of the NOAA ship are present.

All the doctors enter the Conference room and all take a seat. Dr. Wilson introduces the three other members in the room. Dr.Wilson looks at Dr. Hanaka with sad eyes and said.

"Dr. Hanaka we have located some of your crew and all

your students. They all were deceased. The Commanders can give you the details." Dr.Wilson said.

As she is given the news she breaks down crying and sobbing. She is comforted by Brandy and Robert.

She screams out. "It should have been me not my students and crew I am so ashamed of being alive instead..." She is interrupted buy Dr. Wilson.

"Doctor, you could have never known that there was going to be a tsunami and the events that followed. Dr. Wilson concludes.

"Thank you Dr. Wilson, when can I return to Japan." She ask.

The NOAA Captain speaks up, we will be in Oahu tomorrow. Dr. Wilson will arrange the rest."

"We will fly you home immediately with all your dead. It is too dangerous right now because of the after shocks Doctor." said Dr. Wilson.

"I understand." The doctor replies.

"Could the other Commanders tell me what happened to our ship and what exactly happened to the ships crew." The doctor ask.

"Yes, Your ship was located on the beach north of here. On the island and that is the area where your personnel have been located. But that's not to say that some could have survived. We haven't located all of them yet. The Coast Guard is looking for them along with Japan's Coast Guard who arrived this morning Dr.Hanaka" The Coast Guard Commander said.

Upon arrival in Pearl Harbor, Oahu ambulance are waiting on the dock for those crew members that were injured during the title waves.

As Brandy, Jing and Robert drive home they look at each other and Brandy said.

"You know guys we were very lucky to have survived the waves, that whole thing my God…." Brandy is interrupted by Robert.

"You are right, we almost died, but we have survived and now we are going home together with our two wonderful friends Fat Cat and sleepy Ariel and our little girl Jingle Bells. They all laugh.

Ariel climbs onto the car seat and licks Robert in the ear.

"Stop it Ariel, Hay hon. how about stopping and getting some beer and of course Pepsi for Jing and lets catch some surf this afternoon guys." Robert tells them.

"Didn't you get enough surf in Japan." Brandy laughs and ask.

"Well, yes, that was more than surf, but it might have been fun ridding one of those real big waves. How about that beer." Robert ask.

"Ok, I can just see you trying to ride one of them, lets stop at Denys' store." Brandy replies.

"Sure." I need to talk to him anyway Dad, we are going out this coming weekend I think." Jing replied.

Sitting out on the Lanai they all discuss the recent life threatening experiences they all endured.

"So where do we go with this Mermaid search you guys? using the data we have now." Brandy ask.

"I really don't know right now, but I can tell you this I do not want to put us at risk that we just experienced in Japanese islands. We could have died very easily." Robert tells Brandy.

"You are right, we could have died and the program

might have died with you and me. We need to rethink how we approach these Mermaids and where we try and make contact. I just think they have been living in the ocean for thousands of years and have chosen places were people or human like us don't go, even fishermen and especially tourist." Jing said.

"So you think that all of the past events were started or because the Mermaids caused them." Robert ask.

"I don't know how they could have done all that but as scientist we have encouraged more bizarre stuff." Brandy said.

"Maybe we should take advantage of the Mermaids we have right here in the islands and do this research on our own with anyone knowing other than the boss. I just think the Mermaids might have felt so much stress from all of us somehow they caused the shift in the earth using all the fish and manuals in the ocean. I just don't know how they caused these event but they have survived thousands of years. We have almost destroyed the entire earth with our testing of weapons, oil, plastic bottles and fishing gear." Robert replies.

"I need another beer, me too Brandy said."

"I will get the beers for you guys, Jing said.

"You know I am really tired, if I take a nap for an hour wake me up and then lets catch some waves and eat out tonight at Boars Breath. What do you guys think." Robert ask.

"Sounds good, here's your beer drink up and take your nap. I am going to sleep right here." Brandy tells Robert. "I am going into my room I have to make some calls and maybe a short nap. Jing said.

At dinner that night at the Boars Breath, they again start talking about doing there research with the Mermaids alone with out all the different agencies and there ships and personnel. "So what do you think babe." Robert ask as he eats his BQ pork ribs, corn on the cob, cold slaw and several slices of French bread and hot pork and beans.

I well tell you after I stop eating, this stuff is wonderful." Brandy tells Robert. Jing speaks up. "How can you guys eat all that animal flesh, bad you know."

"You go ahead and eat lettuce and soon you will turn into a Rabbit." Robert laughs

On the way home Robert ask Brandy again what she thought about doing the research on their own.

"I like the idea but I am concerned about our safety. What happens if we get one of those male or female Mermaids who do not want us around them or feels threatened. We would not have a chance and could be injured or killed. I like the idea of just you me and Jing doing the actual research but I think we should have our own security force with us if we need them and I think the boss will go alone with us in light of what has happened to Dr. Hanaka of Japan, her staff. I received an e mail today from her and they have elected not to pursue any further investigation of Mermaids. So that leaves us to do the research on our own." Brandy replies.

After dinner both Robert, Jing and Brandy paddle out to the end of the lagoon to catch some waves before retiring that night. While sitting on their boards a Male Mermaid swims up and puts his arm with his web hands over the front of Jing's board and just turns and looks at Brandy. She is somewhat startled but she keeps her composure.

Robert is feeling defensive but keep his distance and his

cool. "The male Merman telepathically tells Brandy that the old Mermaid wants to talk with her the next sun rise. That we must come to their cave as it is safe there. They know about the monster waves and need help

from the monsters of the deep." The Merman tells Brandy.

Brandy looks at him and replies. "We will be there at the next sun rise to help you."

Brandy tells him. The Merman looks at Jing and smiles with his sharp teeth then leaves her surf board and heads to the deep ocean to travel over to the Big Island. The Mermaids and Mermen lives off shore from the County Park in La Po hoe hoe.

Brandy looks at Robert. "Can you believe what just happened". She ask.

"No, what did he say to you, I could not hear the waves were to loud." Robert ask.

"The old Mermaid wants to talk with me tomorrow morning after sun rise he told me." Brandy said. "Did he say anything to you Jing, I saw him smile at you with his sharp teeth, maybe he likes you Jing." Robert laughs.

"Lets paddle in and call the boss." Brandy tells everyone.

Robert, Jing and Brandy paddle in after catching a wave. In the mean time Dr. Wilson is at home BQ with his family and swimming in his pool while his older son does the BQ.

The phone rings and his wife bring s him the phone.

"Hello, yes this is Dr. Wilson, is that you Robert, ok, what's up, no kidding, O my God, They really came all that way, ok I will have security, the boat and personnel will be ready at midnight and we will sell to the Big Island and be in place by sun rise tomorrow. See you at the ship in Pearl."

Dr. Wilson concludes. He continues calling staff members to get the ship ready to sell to the Big Island at midnight.

At the docks, Brandy, Jing and Robert show up at 11:30 pm and Dr. Wilson is standing at the gang plank waiting.

"Good evening doctors, our aid will take your bags and the staff will bring up your diving gear. "Who is taking care of Ariel and Fat Cat." Dr. Wilson ask.

"ToTo our neighbor." Jing answers.

Please follow me to the conference room." Dr. Wilson ask.

Brandy, Jing and Robert look at each other and smile and follow Dr. Wilson. Inside the conference room only the three of them sit down to discuss each other concerns and develop a plan of action with the Mermaids.

"I don't quite understand why and how the Mermaids knew you two were home and about all the events in the Japanese islands. But I think from a scientific view this is once in a lifetime event and if we are ever going to protect this species we must take advantage of this request to meet with them. Now what are your concerns." Dr. Wilson ask.

Our concerns is that all the support teams, ships and personnel in the water makes this species nervous and they some how cause certain events to occur." Brandy said.

"Like, the earth quake, title waves, is that what you think doctor's." Dr. Wilson ask.

"Yes we thought of the same thing doctor, we don't quite understand how but we think they were so stressed by our presents that they set in motion the events that occurred. We just don't want our own population of Mermaids off the Big Island to feel that same way. During our meeting with them in Japan both of us could tell they were getting up tight and very nervous so we cut everything short then all hell broke lose. Yes we are both on the same page with you Dr. Wilson." Robert concludes.

"Anything you want to add Brandy." He ask.

"The only thing I would like to add is I would like us all to take it very slow and discuss what their concerns are and ask them how do they see us helping them. In other words how can humans help protect all Mermaids around the world and in all oceans." Brandy said.

"How do you know they want protection from us or anyone." Dr. Wilson ask.

"I don't know if they need protection from us, when they asked to meet with us the male Mermaid said we need some help from all of you. The old women will meet you at sunrise tomorrow in the cave. I just don't know until we meet." Brandy replies.

"Ok. Your back up will be our security personnel only and I did not notify the Navy or Coast Guard or any other agency. The reason for not notifying these other agency is if the theory that these Mermaids can or cause a catastrophic events that we just experienced in Japan when they feel threatened then we need to change our behaviors so that such events do not occur. In any case we have the security to back both of you doctors up for any event that might occur." Dr. Wilson explained.

"If our theory is that some how the Mermaids call upon the ocean's mammals to cause Hugh waves to occur and some how they also cause a shift in tectonic plates under the water. It is only a theory or just some thought at this point in our research but I agree we need to take it slow and keep as many personnel out of the picture until we either need them or have some how proven our theory." Brandy tells Dr. Wilson

We will be at the shelf next to La Pahoa Hoe in about twenty five minutes. Maybe you guys should start to get ready for your dive and I will get our staff ready to back you two up on the dive. Our security staff will also be ridding the new Sea Bob's but will remain at a distance away from you both but within hearing distance. If either of you feel threatened just say the word Security and the troops will be coming." Dr. Wilson smiled.

Now in front of the La Pohoe Hoe area of the Big Island the NOAA ship sits about one mile off shore out of the way of barges going to Hilo and delivering goods for the Big island and out of the path of cruse ships with hundreds of tourist coming and going to the Big Island.

Inside the cabin they get into their wet suites and play with Fat Cat and Brandy's pug Sleepy Ariel. Jing knocks on the door and joins them as they walk to the dive room lower deck.

Soon they meet with the launching team on the lower deck away from wondering eyes as they enter the water on their sleds followed by security staff.

As Brandy, Jing and Robert head towards the entrance of the cave, dolphins swim along side in a playful manor when two Merman come swimming along side of the Sea

Bob and hang on to the sled for a free ride with one hand and spears in the other hand.

Brandy looks over and smiles at both of them. Both send her a message. "We ride with you today." Brandy sends a message back. "You ride."

Soon Brandy, Jing and Robert arrive in the same inlet

area they meet before. The older women is again surrounded by other younger female Mermaids. This time Brandy looks around to see if any boats or ships could see them and ask Robert.

"Robert, look around and see if anyone could sneak up on us or see us before we take off our mask. I do not want to put our friends here at risk ok." Brandy ask.

Robert pulls himself up on the rocks and looks around.

"I can not see any boats or person within miles." Robert replies.

"Ok lets take off our mask, you too Jing." Brandy orders.

The older Mermaid opens her mouth as if she was going to say something but only shows her sharp teeth, perhaps in a jester of pleasure. Brandy returns the jester and smiles with all her teeth showing. All Mermaids pat the water making a jester of clapping as if the water was a second hand and they liked what Brandy just did and Brandy, Jing and Robert picks up on it and pats the water with their hands. Brandy now knows a behavior that is accepted by the Mermaids when they like something like Brandy showing all her teeth in response to the old women showing her teeth.

The old Mermaid moves close to Brandy, Jing and Robert steps back to give her room to be next to them. She looks into Brandy's eyes with her scary black eyes and tells Brandy telepathy.

"My friend, people like me in far away islands were very threatened by so many humans in the water they called upon all the Mermaids in the waters to raise the ocean waves to get ride of them and so it was done. We need your help to keep humans away from our people because humans carry diseases and kill our people with high pitch noises. Only someone like you can save our people. We have been dying by the hundreds. The shark has always been our enemy but now humans have become our number one enemy. Please help us."

The old Mermaid tells Brandy without saying a word, now all the Mermen and Mermaids look at Brandy waiting for an answer.

Brandy looks at Jing and Robert for support. Jing understands what was said as does Robert and he nods his head as to say go ahead I am here to support you, tell me what you want me to do to help you.

Brandy turns back to the old Mermaid and ask her telepathically "You have told me that humans are your enemy. Please tell me what do humans do besides the high pitch machines, how do they kill your people." Brandy ask.

The water erupts with all the Mermen and Mermaids pounding on the water with their fist wanting to tell Brandy how humans kill them and then the old Mermaid raises her fin like hand and all becomes calm in the water. She again looks Brandy into the eyes she turns to Jing and tells her. "They kill our people with Hugh nets, putting many dead fish into the water bring our enemy sharks who eat our young. They put plastic bags in the waters and our young suffocate on them. Human ships put garbage into the water and bring more sharks who kill our young. Your warriors drop many bombs into the water for years and killed off most all our people. Ships put oil and other chemicals into the water and it chocks our people to death. You and Robert and your daughter Jing can help us but can you tell us why you humans use the ocean as a dumping grounds.' She ask.

Jing looks at the old Mermaid in the eye and tells her.

"I think our warriors do the testing of bombs to scare off our enemies, I think humans that dump stuff into all the waters do so because they can. It is a big ocean and the ships that dump into the ocean do so because they can get away with it, Jing concludes.

Again the waters erupt with Mermaids and Merman pounding the waters in protest of what Jing has just telepathically said. Again the old women raises her hand to stop them.

"I don't have all the answers you are looking for but I have some of them." Brandy said.

As Jing pointed out, our Navy was testing a machine that sends our low frequency through the water and it resulted in many deaths and our leaders have stopped it. The old Mermaid looks at Brandy and tells her. "No they haven't, our people in other waters told us they continue killing our people." The old Mermaid replies.

Brandy replies, "I will look into this for you."

"Also I know many humans drop plastic bags into the water along with other items and it is killing your people and fish in the ocean. We are working to stop it. No more bombing in the south pacific in fifty years. Brandy tells her. She nods her head as yes.

"In order to protect all your people in the waters of the world I need you to share how all of you communicate. I know you told me some of it last time we meet, but I need to know and understand how we are talking without using words. You teach me how you do this and I will help all your people." Brandy replies.

The old women nods her head. She points at her eyes and tells Brandy.

"You must first learn to look humans in the eye up close. When we first learned how to talk in the water we still grunted, then we were able to enter each others mind. The eyes are the gateway into the mind. By looking into the eyes of each other we start to communicate with each other. I enter your mind you enter mine. Later we learned how to communicate with our friends the Dolphins and what you call Whales."

The old Mermaids directs a young girl Mermaid to come next to Jing and look her in the eyes and communicate with her. The young little girl sat next to Jing and smiled. Even this little girl had sharp teeth like a shark. Brandy looked her in the eyes and communicated.

"My Name is Jing what is yours." Jing ask telepathically.

"They call me Ella." She replies.

"Ok Ella how did you learn to talk without words." Jing ask.

"If we talked with words the sharks will come and eat us." Ella tells Jing.

Jing smiles and looks over at Brandy. Robert smiles and shakes his head and looks at Brandy in the eyes and for the first time communicates with her telepathy.

"Hay babe can you believe this, they are so smart and have developed how to Communicate telepathy. She is so cute. Robert replies.

Brandy smiles and turn to Ella and ask. "What name do your people call your self's like we humans call you Mermaids and the Mermen." Brandy looks at Ella in the eyes.

"We call each other by our names and have never called our self's other names. I guess we are Mermaids and Mermen as a people of the water but each of us are different like you two are different from other humans.

"Ok Ella I need you to help me learn how to communicate with you without talking verbally, you know no words, just looking at each other and talking like we are right now." Brandy ask.

"Sure, we are talking right now without saying a word like humans, It comes natural when you first learn how to talk to each other. We had to learn how to communicate this way because we needed a way to talk under water and our people started communicating under water and just continued on top of the water." Ella tells Brandy.

Ok, I see how you now communicate with each other and me but how do you communicate over a long distance Ella." Brandy ask.

"Our warm blooded friends, you call whales sing songs that travel many miles then other whales sign the same song until it arrives at the place where it was sent and that is how we send messages or you call communications." said Ella.

"Ok, we will do everything within our power to help all of you. Please come and visit us in the waves when we are surfing in front of our home." Brandy tells the entire group of Mermaids and Mermen. Jing put her arm around Ella and the entire pod of Mermaids and Mermen erupt in apploding her. Brandy, Jing and Robert put on their mask and soon return to their ship on the Sea bob's. They all return to their cabin and change their clothes without incident. Soon they meet with Dr. Wilson in the conference room for a debriefing. As Brandy, Jing and Robert enter the conference room they each have their pet in their arms, Sleepy Ariel and Fat Cat. Dr. Wilson speaks up.

"I thought you left your children at home with ToTo."

"ToTo had to go to work for her grandpa in the store today. Robert said.

"I thought you two would come with your children so I ordered food for them right over here."

Dr. Wilson pointing to an area in the corner that has a pail of dog food and cat food and separate bowls of water. "Thank you doctor I will let Ariel give you a big kiss for that food." Brandy smiles and sits down at the conference table and lets Ariel go eat. Brandy and Robert look at Dr. Wilson waiting for the meeting to start.

"Ok, we recorded the conversations you had with the girl Ella, the eye camera captured all areas of the eye and doctors are researching them now in hopes they can understand the communications Brandy." "So do you communicate with them now. How does it work." Dr. Wilson ask.

Look it is simple Doctor. Move over buy me and now look me in the eyes and start thinking of words you want to communicate with me, that's it you are telling me you want to learn how to talk with Mermaids, I received your words, now continue and now listen to my words Doctor." Brandy continues.

"O my God, I did not think it was so easy to communicate by telepathy with someone. I guess some people think it is mind reading of some sort, but I know that the eyes are the gateway to one's mind and the Mermaids and Mermen have mastered this way of communicating. It is very important that we all keep this encounter with Ella secret from other agencies. The reason for this is we need to get our contacts in congress and the President on board with our findings and legislation and orders to stop any further research by the

Navy and then develop a plan that all countries can work together cleaning up our oceans all over the world without endangering our friends the Mermaids and Mermen." Dr. Wilson concludes.

"What can we do to help you Doctor." Brandy ask.

"Nothing right now, just don't tell anyone about our discovery and our plan of action. You two take a well deserved week off while I fly to D.C. and meet with our people." Dr. Wilson said.

"Can we take one of the Sea Bob's home with us to vacation on Doctor." Brandy ask.

"Not a chance, unless you assign both of your paychecks over to me." Dr.Wilson laughs. Robert, Jing and Brandy get up from the conference table and take their children with them back to the cabin.

Inside the Cabin Robert ask Jing and Brandy. "So what do we do now for the next week. Do you want to go anywhere like travel or just hang out around the house and rest."

"I just want to hang out and sleep and eat out every night and surf during the day and take naps in the afternoon." Jing tells them. "Sounds good to me." Brandy and Robert answer.

That evening while Jing, Brandy and Robert drive to dinner, just as they back out of there driveway and heads towards town. A Merman's head pops up as the wave breaks. He is looking at the doctors drive away.

At dinner that night Brandy, Jing and Robert are discussing issues about their new found friends Ella, the old Mermaid and all the Mermaids and Mermen.

"I think we need to get some rest first, some surfing and

then all sit down and write down some type of plan for our country and other countries that will follow our lead and then we might have a chance in meeting the Mermaids and Mermen request and they will survive." Jing said.

"That is a real good suggestion Jing."

"Well we have a few days off and we did bring a Sea Bob home with us, how about checking out the Mermaid population around Oahu." Brandy ask.

"That sounds real good but we have to very careful around all the military facilities, they all have sound security systems, maybe we should limit the search to north shore area, what do you think." Robert ask.

"That is probably not a good idea, remember there is a Marine Corp. Base. If the doctor found out, well you know he would be really upset with us. Let's just have fun with the Sea Bob." Brandy suggest.

The next morning Robert hooks up the Sea Bob and waits for Brandy and Jing to help him launch the Sea Bob. It looks like a Sea Doo but has seating for two and tanks. The electric motors propels the Sea Bob through the water with ease. The driver has a steering wheel to direct them. Brandy directs Robert as he backs down the ramp with the Sea Bob. Jing heads out to the surf with her friends. Soon Brandy and Robert are headed out to the shelf along the ocean shore going north up cost. The water in so clear as they watch a pod of doffing swim with them. A very large Manna ray swims by to say hello. They are down about fifty feet in the water when a strong current grabs them. In the current the Sea Bob is tossed around like a toy. Robert is struggling with the controls. He soon get control and they leave the current to the ocean below.

"How about heading home we have no control out here and no support." Robert ask Brandy.

"No problem, lets go home." Brandy tell Robert.

After returning home Robert and Brandy head to Perl Harbor and return the Sea Bob to the NOAA ship.

The next week both of them are in meetings all week teaching other agencies how to telepathy communicate. While meeting with Dr. Wilson called the doctors into his office and said.

"How was your ride on the Sea Bob, you two don't think we would spend so much money on these without having a GPS on them We knew you two were going to have fun with it. Now go teach the other agencies." Dr. Wilson smiles. Brandy, Jing and Robert look at each other and smile.

In the meeting, one of the staff members receives a message that a Hugh earthquake just occurred in Japan and a tsunami is likely to hit the Hawaiian islands in one hour. Robert looks at Brandy and both of them said at the same time,

"Ariel and Fat Cat." they both said.

Soon both of them are heading home to rescue their children. As they head home the tsunami sirens start up and everyone on the island starts moving high up the hills away from the Ocean. As Brandy gathers the dog and cats food, along with extra water and their dishes. Robert yells out.

"Lets get out of here, it is starting the water is getting pulled out, lets go now, I have both children in the car."

"I am in the car." as Brandy enters and they speed off down the highway past Hale'wa Beach Park and head through the town to the freeway. Brandy looks towards the beach and recalls the strong currents they both experienced last week at Laniakea Turtle Beach.

Soon they are looking at the freeway and it is bumper to bumper, they look at each other and head up the steepest road they can see, Brandy and Jing are looking out the window and they see a Hugh wave about sixty feet high towards north shore. They park in a cult sack and get out of the car and run to the cliff and look at the approaching wave. As the wave gets close to the shore the wave starts building with the accumulation of water from the shoreline. As it crashes down on the shore a Hugh roaring noise pounds the shore line, as if bombs were dropped on the shore. The ocean water does not stop there, it rushes inland like a freight train roaring every foot and destroying everything in it's path. Tearing homes apart, throwing cars into the air like a baseball. Across the highway and stopping at the hillside. They know there are more to come and fear for anyone in low line areas could be at risk of drowning.

For the next hour smaller waves hit the shore adding to the already damaged homes, cars and building in the small towns in the path. Soon the all clear siren signals for all to return to the shoreline. Everyone including Brandy, Jing and Robert take their time driving slow close to the shoreline. Brandy, Jing and Robert are felling anxiety about their home being hit by the tsunami.

"Do you think we have a home to return to." Jing ask.

Where we were on the mountain I could not see our cove where we live so I do not know if the wave got us. We soon will find out Jing." Robert tells her.

As they drive by the little town and homes that use to face the ocean they are gone, wood, debris and cars pilled up everywhere. Total destruction alone the shoreline and very difficult to drive even though they have a Toyota 4X4 not knowing where the road is at times with mud, sand and debris everywhere. Soon they are at their cove and their home is gone. All that sits on the spot where there home was is trees that have been striped clean as if someone had cut every leaf off the trees. There was a path leading from where their home back across the highway and up part of the hillside. Their home is scattered over a mile from the shoreline. Brandy looks at where their homes use to be and burst out crying. Robert try's to comfort her but it was indeed a shock for all of them. They stop, get out where their homes once stood and Robert tells Brandy.

"We will rebuild babe, don't worry we are insured for this. We will build a beautiful home just the way you want ok." Robert tries to comfort Brandy and Jing.

"I know babe, but we lost all our personal stuff, pictures, awards, clothes all the little stuff we accumulated over a life time. I guess it will be fun building the type of home we always wanted with a beautiful Lanai and open kitchen. I thought we might be safe living across the street from the ocean but it really does not matter when that wave comes in. It was so powerful, you would have to live up on the mountain to be safe." Brandy tells Robert.

"We will have fun building but in the mean time we need to find somewhere to live with Jing and our other children. Thank God they are ok and no one got hurt. So what do you think about living in Government housing close to Perl until we rebuild." Robert ask Brandy.

"Are you talking about the guest housing NOAA has in Perl." Ask Brandy.

"Yes I will call Dr. Wilson and get the ok and then we will go shopping for clothes and the basics babe." Robert said.

"Do you think Perl suffered and damage from this tsunami, I hope there is housing to move into." Brandy replies.

"Not to worry, it's ringing now Dr. Wilson is answering the phone."

"Dr. Wilson here."

"Dr. Wilson our home is no more, it's gone. Do you have housing for us doctor." Ask Robert.

"Yes of course, you two move into one of our guest homes on the island next to the golf course, I will call security and have them assist you two I am so sorry about your house.

No the tsunami did not effect Perl, thank God, I knew you were about to ask that question. Right now Robert I am on one of our boats heading north to help the Coast Guard assess the damage. You two eat at my house tonight with my family, say 7pm, ok Robert." Dr. Wilson said.

"See you their doctor and thank you." Robert replies.

Robert puts his arm around Jing and Brandy to comfort them while standing on what use to be there home and said.

"We have one of guest homes next to golf course and on the lagoon. Perl did not get any damage and we are eating at the bosses tonight." Robert tells them. Jing speaks up.

"Do you guys realize we can paddle out to the north shore from our new house and surf. Is that cool or what." She said.

Brandy looks up at Robert and smiles with relief. The

rest of the day was spent buying clothing and food for their temporary home in Perl.

That evening after dinner at Dr. Wilson's residence Brandy and Robert walk out onto lanai looking down Waikiki and the ocean.

"I have to tell you both I thank God neither of you were injured during the tsunami today. I know your home was destroyed. You two can live in the residence as long as you need to. I have to let all of you know that the President her self is very interested in the Mermaids and will give us all the support we need. However we do have some individuals in the Navy, mainly certain Admirals that do not want us to go foreword because it will stop their programs. Again lets keep our plans to ourselves only." Dr. Wilson said. "Thank you doctor, we will." Robert tells him.

"Did you get a chance to talk with the President doctor." Brandy ask.

"I did and she assured me that her staff and her will support our research and she requested we keep our finding to ourself and her Chief of Staff only at this time.

Brandy, Jing and Robert return to their home on the golf course and lagoon sitting on the lanai with Fat Cat and sleepy Ariel. They sit quite petting their children trying to calm themselves from the horrible day they both experienced with the destruction of their home, the shock of returning and seeing everything they have together destroyed. Robert has called there insurance agent and he has reassured them that they are covered for their losses.

Brandy ask Robert, "So what do you think happened to our friends off the Big island after the tsunami."

"I don't think they got hit by the wave according to

our research ship in the area. Captain Dean told me this afternoon that the wave did not hit the Big Island. Thank God eh." Robert said. "Right, but I still would like to check in on them." Brandy replies.

"You can't mother them Brandy, they have survived these waters long before man was here and…." Robert was telling Brandy when the phone rang. Robert answers the phone it is Dr. Wilson.

"Hi Robert I would like you three to accompany me to Washington and meet with the President tomorrow. Meet me at the Tar mat at 0500 hrs. Talk with you later." Dr. Wilson hangs up the phone.

"Can you believe that babe, Dr. Wilson ordered us to meet him at 05:00 hrs tomorrow and fly with him to DC and meet with the President."

"How cool is that." Robert said.

The next morning Brandy, Jing and Robert board the private jet and fly to Washington DC and meet with the President and some of her staff that are scientist. They meet with the President in one of the side offices to keep a low profile around staff members they were told by the Chief of Staff.

They had a twenty minute meeting with the President and she assured all of them that her administration would support their research. In the meeting was the Secretary of Defense and she assured all of them her department would put in place support systems that would protect the Mermaids in our oceans. Also in attendance was the Security of State. She spoke up and told Dr. Wilson.

"Doctor you and your staff can be assured that my office will seek out other countries who are friendly and supportive of our goals to put in place rules that protect these Mermaids. After all they seem to be the oldest humans on earth. They appear to have survived some of the worst changes on our planet and I share our Presidents view that these species deserve our support.

"Thank you Madam Security." Brandy and Jing replies.

"Yes thank you Madam Security." They all reply.

The President walked over Brandy, Jing and Robert and she said.

"You doctors are doing work that will at some point will help millions of people world wide will benefit from, but for now we need to keep this information classified to protect our knowledge from those who might take advantage of this population. We simply need to protect and study these folks right." She ask.

"Yes indeed Madam President." Brandy, Jing and Robert reply.

Robert, Jing and Brandy with Dr. Wilson fly back to Oahu. Nine hours later they arrive. All are very tried and soon are asleep with the light trade winds help all the doctors sleep through out the night. The next morning after breakfast Brandy, Jing and Robert head to north shore to catch some surf. Despite the damage to homes close to the beach, In a local board shop all three pick out a new board with three scags. They go to the park, wax the boards and head out to the surf. While sitting on their surf boards Brandy tells Robert.

"I feel so sorry for everyone who lost their home but life continues and they have their lives like us. Do you think any bodies are in the surf or like homes." Brandy ask.

"No, there has been enough time laps so don't worry

about that lets just have some fun and catch some waves and relax today babe." Robert replies.

While sitting on her surf board Jing feel a hand tugging on her leg. She looks over her board on the right side and see's her friend the old Mermaid looking up at her.

Jing looks her in the eyes and said. "Are you ok after the big wave. How are your people and the children." Brandy ask the old women,

"We all are ok, we have seen these types of waves many times. When they are coming we go out into the open ocean so we do not get hit by the big wave. Your ships do the same thing. We looked and your home is gone so we looked for you on your wooden boards that ride the waves and we found you. Are your leaders going to stop the ships with the noise that kills our young and our people." She ask... Brandy.

"Yes, our leader said she will stop there noise in our countries waters but they will have to get the other countries to agree. It is like getting other Mermaid tribes to agree. So all your people within two hundred miles of our shoreline will be protected and our people will protect your people in our waters. We can not kill your enemy the shark because the ocean needs the shark but we can protect your people other ways." Brandy answers her.

Robert paddles over to where Brandy is and realizes she is meeting with the old

Mermaid. "Oh I did not know you two were talking, I saw you looking down and wanted to see what you were looking at now I know." Robert tells Brandy and Jing without saying a word. Robert can now communicate in the Mermaids telepathic way of communicating.

There were several other surfers in the area and Brandy tells the old women one thing they need to do is protect them from the locals so they do not explode them or tell others where they are. Brandy ask the old Mermaid.

"Have you moved after the big wave." Brandy ask.

"Yes all our people have moved to those rocks at the end of the canal where you, Jing and Robert now live." She tells Brandy while leaning over the surf board away from the view of others.

Brandy is a little shocked that the Mermaids are so smart and able to figure out where her and Robert live and want to live close. Actually Brandy is flattered that they want to live close to her and Robert. Soon the old women disappears into the ocean with others waiting in the waves. Brandy paddles with Jing next to Robert and tells him.

"Can you believe how smart they are."

"I knew they were smart because they have survived for many centuries but I had no idea how smart. I feel like their protector or part of their tribe. Some how this commitment by them raises our commitments to their tribe." Robert tells Brandy.

"I agree and I feel the same way." Brandy replies. "Me too." Jing replies.

While driving home Robert and Brandy discuss their encounter with the Mermaids and agree the encounter raises their commitment to them up a notch. As they drive by the rocky area at the mouth of their canal they both look and now know the Mermaids are living among the Hugh rocks protecting their young and the rest of the tribe. Brandy turns to Robert and said.

"Just having the knowledge that the tribe of Mermaids

are at the end of our canal makes me feel very good. Like we have really connected with this tribe and we must protect them with every fiber of our self's." Brandy said.

"I agree babe." Robert replies.

"Now the question is how do we do that without everyone knowing what we are doing." Brandy ask.

"I think we start by restricting all boat traffic from coming into their area. That can be accomplished by having Fish and Game on our team. This way, no will know that we are behind the movement and won't ask questions of any of our personnel. Like Dr. Wilson said we need to limit what our mission is to even our staff because everything gets leaked sooner or later. If we can keep our plans to a small group we have a chance to protect our Mermaids that surround the Pacific." Robert replies.

"let's meet with Dr. Wilson and share our ideas. What do you think Robert." Brandy ask

"Lets do it."

Soon Brandy and Robert are meeting with Dr. Wilson in his office. Dr. Wilson closes his door and the meeting proceeds. After Robert and Brandy share there ideas on how to implement the plan to protect these Mermaids Dr. Wilson said.

"I like your ideas and I have also had a conversation with the Commander of the Coast Guard. They are going to form a small group of Seamen to guard, and enforce the safety zone for our friends. Is there any other support we could provide" Dr. Wilson ask.

"I don't think so, but I will check with them and get back to you." Brandy replies.

Brandy and Robert are soon in the water at the mouth

of their Lagoon looking for their new friends the Mermaids. The water is so clear and nice and deep with large boulders to hind in and protect the Mermaids. There is a large bed of kelp coming up from the bottom which provides a good place to hide from there enemy the Shark. Soon Brandy and Robert are meet by a contingency of Mermen. Brandy and Robert follow them to the bottom of a Hugh rock and swim up from the middle of the rock into an area Surrounded by rock and sand and fresh air.

Brandy and Robert remove there mask and are greeted by the old women and her trough of young Mermaids. She looks at Brandy and telepathically tell her they like there new safe place away from the sharks and boat people with their nets, the boats with noise, the Navy with their low frequency noise machines Brandy replied.

"You now know my mate Robert and my daughter Jing we live on the canal. We are going to do several things to protect all your people. Our people are going to keep all boats away from this are at lease three mile into the ocean. No diving zone, meaning no one can dive here. No fishing in this area, leaving all the fish for your people. We will have our people around here to enforce these new laws, the boats in the area will be friendly to all Mermaids. What else do your people need." Brandy ask the old women.

"We need to be able to get in touch with you my dear when you are in your cave. I realize you leave sometimes but we have no other way to get in touch with you other than wait until you are on your board." The old Mermaid said.

"Robert will set up some type of rope your Merman can pull and it will ring a bell inside our cave and we will go into the water and meet with you." Brandy replies.

"When will you do this." The old Mermaid ask.

"Today, Brandy replies.

The old Mermaid looks into Brandy eyes and smiles and said.

"Thank you."

That afternoon Dr. Wilson called Brandy's home.

"I know you doctors are visiting the Mermaids at the rocks at the end of the lagoon and that is wonderful but I want to be kept in the loop of everything you guys agree to or do with them. Understood." he said.

"Understood doctor." Brandy replies.

"In regards to that we have agreed to put in place some type of string and a bell to get our attention when they need to see us." Robert tells Dr. Wilson.

"Great, I will have someone from maintenance out to your home within the hour. This is the type of stuff the President wants to be informed with. Thank you doctors." He concludes.

The next couple days are uneventful until that evening when the bell rings non stop.

Brandy and Robert run to the canal and see two Merman looking at Jing. She yells over to Robert who is just getting out of his Toyota. The two Merman motion for Robert, Jing and Brandy to follow them. Brandy walks to the edge of the water and she tells them.

"We have to get our tanks on and we will follow on the underwater Sea Bob. You two can ride with us." Brandy concludes.

Without having to discuss what is happening Robert calls Dr. Wilson and advises that the Mermaids have requested to see them right a way. Brandy and Jing run and get there tanks, mask and fins and run to the dock and lower both Sea Bobs into the water. They Look down the lagoon underwater and some of the neighbors are sitting in there yard and catch a glimpse of the two Mermen hanging onto the Sea Bobs in amusement. Soon they are at the rock cave of all the Mermaids and Mermen. Brandy, Jing and Robert remove there mask and the old Mermaid swims up to Brandy and looks her in her eyes and said.

"You promised the Navy would not use their ships to send radio waves in the water that kill our people and friends." She continues to look into Brandy's eyes waiting for an answer. Brandy looks over at Robert hoping he has some information about what the old Mermaid is talking about. Brandy looks into the old women's eyes and said.

"I did give you my promise that the Navy would not do that again. Show me what they have done." Brandy ask.

"Lets take a ride on your machine." She tells Brandy then turns to the entire pod and orders them to stay in the cave.

As Brandy, Jing and Robert head out to the ocean and open waters with Mermen and the old Mermaid hanging onto Brandy Sea Bob as they travel under water they soon see a pod of dolphins floating in the water that have died, bleeding from the ears just like the dolphins that died in the 2001 (IMP) Interference Mitigation program of the Navy active Sonar programs. Brandy looks over at the old women and shacks her head in disbelief. Within seconds they come upon hundreds of fish and sharks dead in the water and sitting in the horizon is an unmarked ship with no numbers but bearing the Navy stripes around the smoke stacks. It is the (LFA) ship, Frequency Active Sonar Brandy tells the old women. Brandy motions to Robert to turn around to head back but as they turn to return to the rock caves to drop off the old women so they can go into the office and talk with Dr. Wilson of their findings the Merman brake away from the Sea Bob's and coming up from the kelp beds are hundreds of Merman with spears heading towards the Navy ship. The old women turns to Brandy and tells her.

"I can't stop them, they want blood, they know you promised but many times humans have promised to protect us only to take advantage of us and then kill us. The Mermen will not stop until they kill the humans on the bad ship." She tells Brandy.

Robert motions to Brandy and Jing to return and drop off the old women then they can try and stop the attack on the ship from home.

Within minutes they drop off the Old Mermaid and drive there Sea Bob onto the dock lift on the canal. They run into the house to call Dr. Wilson.

Within seconds Robert is on the phone with Dr. Wilson.

"Dr. Wilson you need to call the Navy and warn there Sonar ship at sea that Mermen are about to attack them." Robert blurts out.

"What in the world are you talking about Robert, the Navy has agreed not to continue that Sonar program. The Admiral told the President that…."he is interrupted by Robert.

"If you don't notify them some innocent people might get hurt. Do it right now doctor and then we will talk. I do not know who to contact and you do." Robert tells Dr. Wilson.

"Alright Robert I will call them but I hope you are right

and we don't get embarrassed over this Robert. I will call you right back. Dr. Wilson concludes.

In the mean time hundreds of Mermen are heading towards the Navy ship armed with spears and about thirty of them swimming with a Hugh wooden log. As they approach the ship they shove the Hugh wooden log into the patellar and stop the ship. Part of the brass patellar is bent. No matter what they do they are stuck in the water. Next the Mermen surface next to the ships gangplank and motion the sailors on deck to come down to the gang blank. About eight of them come down to the waters edge and without a word fifty Merman come up out of the water and throw there spears into the body of the seamen. They all die, some fall into the ocean and others die on the gang plank. All Mermen return to the rock caves.

Back at the Navy ship, sailors are removing the bodies from the gang plank putting their bodies into body bags. Off in the distance Naval Seals in there rubber craft are heading towards the ship.

By the time the Navy Seals arrive the Merman are long gone. The Navy Seals board the ship and take up positions around the ship in anticipation of another attack by the Merman. That will not happen. The Mermen fight like our minute men against the British. The navy Seals remain aboard until the tug boats arrive to pull the ship into Pearl Harbor boat yard. The Navy cover the Sonar equipment so the curious eyes will not see anything.

Dr. Wilson ask Brandy, Jing and Robert to meet him in his office right away. Within minutes they are in Dr. Wilson's office at NOAA headquarters. Dr. Wilson tells them...

"The Mermen just attacked a Naval ship and killed eight Naval Seamen. I know they must be retaliating for the SONAR attack on them and their friends..." He is interrupted by Brandy.

"Doctor, Madam President guaranteed us that the Navy would stop these sonar testing and based upon that guarantee I told the Mermaids and Mermen that it would never happen again. Now what do we do." Brandy ask.

"I think we need to call the White House and talk with the Chief of Staff to get some direction on how we should proceed. I will call both of you soon, but in the meantime stay away from the Mermen and Mermaids they could be very dangerous because you broke your promise to them." Dr. Wilson said.

"We will wait for your call doctor." Robert said.

As Brandy, Jing and Robert drive home they discuss the events that occurred today and talk about how to save the Mermaids and Mermen.

"I know the President is going to be pissed, She made an executive order for the NAVY to stand down with the SONAR project. I wonder what is happening, anyway all I know babe is that we have to figure out some plan to either move the Mermaids to a safe area or make sure that Sonar ship is stopped so the Mermaids live in peace and no retaliation against them for the attack on the Navy ship." "How do we do that babe." Brandy ask.

"I think Dr. Wilson needs to call the Chief of Staff at the White House and she can talk with the President about everything. We just can't do nothing. But we need to do something without it firing back into our faces. We need to coordinate our efforts with Dr. Wilson and our entire staff to save our friends." Robert replies.

Robert ends his sentence a call comes in over the NOAA cell phone. Brandy looks down at her cell phone and said.

"It is Dr. Wilson." Brandy said. She put the phone on speaker.

"Ok you doctors, the Chief of Staff just told me that Madam President has fired the Security of the Navy and two Admirals over this incident. She has ordered the Navy to stand down and stop all testing. She has ordered the entire program to be closed down immediately. I just don't know how we re assure the Mermaids that this will never occur again. I just saw picture of over thirty five Dolphins dead on our beaches. I feel so bad about this. Before you two do anything call me and we will discuss it so we can have backup for you guys with our own people ok. I need to go now, don't forget call me first." Dr. Wilson orders.

In the meantime hundreds of Mermen are arriving from all over the ocean. They are getting ready to attack another Navy ship. They want revenge and are discussing this among themselves. Brandy, Jing and Robert drive down to the end of the jetty and look at all the Mermen arriving. It looks like a school of fish but they know it is hundreds of Mermen.

"Robert you were a Navy Seal what would you do in this situation." Brandy ask.

"I think the thing to do is arrive in force just in case, then bring something that will assure them that all the ships have stopped the Sonar testing and they will listen to us I think. We also need the old women on our side. But first we need to call Dr. Wilson before we do anything." Robert told Brandy and Jing.

At home, Robert calls Dr. Wilson and tells him what is going on. Dr. Wilson tells them he will order all his security force to meet them in the canal in thirty minutes. Within twenty five minutes the first in many Sea Bob's arrive in the canal to back up Robert, Jing and Brandy. The security force has decided to hang back just to let the Mermen know they are there but to give the doctors support when arriving at the caves of the Mermaids. Brandy spots the old Mermaid and she motions them to come over to her. The old Mermaid is sitting on the edge of a rock, half in the water and half out. She again motions Brandy to come closer and she does. The old Mermaid looks into Brandy's eye and ask.

"Are your men at war with us." She ask telepathically.

"No, they are her for our safety only." Brandy replies.

The old Mermaid looks away for a minute and turns again and looks into Brandy's eye and tells her.

"You do not have to fear us because you three have been honest with us but what happened with that Navy ship. They killed our friends and some of our children." She tells Brandy and Jing.

"I know what you say is true and our President has ordered again to all such ships to stop the testing. You will never experience this again from our country. I can not guarantee other countries ships. Brandy tell her.

The old women nods her head and motions to the Mermen and they all surfaced and meet in another area around the caves.

Brandy motions to the security staff to back off. They take her lead but only back up a few yards to protect them.

Brandy, Jing and Robert put there mask back on and return to their Sea Bob's and head back up the canal.

After calling Dr. Wilson and briefing him they also address how to keep the Mermaids safe around all our shores of the Pacific Coast and Atlantic Coast. Dr. Wilson suggested…

"We not only need to protect the Mermaids around the Hawaiian Islands but we need to address up and down the Pacific Coast. I received an e mail from the L.A. County Sheriff's Office that Mermaids have been spotted around Catalina in the Kelp beads. My concern again is that there are Navy bases up and down the coat and some of the civilians who were part of the Sonar program could be still operating for the company that received the contract and are being paid by that company despite the Presidents orders to the Navy and…." Dr. Wilson is interrupted by Brandy.

"You mean to tell us that there are runagates still using Sonar killing Mermaids, Dolphins and Whales." Brandy ask.

"Yes, over eight whales and thirty two dolphins have been located in a beach south of Santa Barbara and…" Dr. Wilson is again interrupted by Robert.

"Do we have our ships in the area right now doctor." Robert ask.

"No, I wanted to be there personally with you doctors. We need to conduct the investigation with you doctors. You have twenty minutes to meet me at the tarmac, we are flying to L.A. NOAA now." Dr. Wilson tells them.

Brandy turns to Robert and asked him…"

"Call TuTu to come over here and stay until we return, take care of our children." Brandy orders.

"She is on the way." Robert tells Brandy.

Within minutes all three doctors are at the Tarmac getting onto NOAA jet to L.A.Five and half hours later they arrive at LAX and taxies over to the NOAA hanger. They are meet by staff members of NOAA and helicopter to the beach area just south of Santa Barbara. As there helicopter hovers over the dead whales and Dolphins the NOAA photo Officer taking pictures. Dr. Wilson looks in horror as men in white outfits are taking samples from the dead mammals. He orders the helicopter to land and said.

"All NOAA security personnel stop and detain all those unauthorized personnel on the beach. Do not let them get to their vehicles. Use whatever force is necessary copy." Dr. Wilson orders.

Robert & Jing and Brandy with Dr. Wilson look out the windows of the helicopter. They see men in white overalls running towards their vehicles in the parking lot. They are stopped by an army of NOAA security armed personnel. All of the personnel are stopped, arrested and all the evidence is taken away. All of them are handcuffed and transported to NOAA security offices and interviewed with the assistance of the FBI. Once interviewed they are booked at the Federal Detention down town L.A.

On the beach Brandy, Jing and Robert work with Dr. Wilson examine most of the whales, and dolphins and each one of them were bleeding from the ears and mouth which is congruent with death from Low Frequency Active Sonar. Brandy looks up at Robert and tears are running down her cheeks from sadness of all the dead whales and Daphnis. Brandy turns to Dr. Wilson and ask.

"How can this happen doctor. Madam President ordered

the Sonar testing to stop and…" She is interrupted by Dr. Wilson.

"Brandy a lot of the time when the President orders certain programs to stop like any of the so called black programs it takes time for all the people in charge to order there employees to stop doing what ever they are doing, get the picture. Also there are politics involved so we just have to be patience and those orders will take effect soon.

"So what do we tell the Mermaids." Brandy ask.

"Nothing. We need to do our research on these animals and I will inform the Chief of Staff and await for the President to take action. At that time we will make contact again with the Mermaids. Dr. Wilson replies.

Just then Dr. Wilson turns away from the others and listens to his cell phone. The expression on his face told Brandy and Robert there was something wrong going on as Dr. Wilson turned towards them and said.

"I can not believe what I was told." Dr. Wilson said.

"What is it doctor." Ask Brandy.

"The Navy seals are on their way to attack the Mermen and Mermaids." He reported.

"We need to stop them, but how do we do that doctor." Robert tells Dr. Wilson.

"I am calling the Chief of Staff at the White house and ask him to call the Secutary of the Navy to stop them right now. Dr. Wilson tells Brandy, Jing and Robert. Within a Dr. Roberts reports the Seal Team have stood down and are returning to their ship.

"I was told that there could be one or two renegades that might take some action against our Mermaids, so the Navy is now instructing NCIS to investigate the Seal Team to assure that the Presidents orders are followed to the letter. Also the FBI is investigating because this took place on American waters. Of course the Coast Guard investigators are involved. In the mean time we have a report that a Mermaid body has washed up on the beach at Aogashima Island Japan. Dr. Hamaski is already on the scene and is awaiting our arrival. We will fly to Japan then take our ship that is awaiting us in the harbor." Dr. Wilson tells Brandy, Jing and Robert.

While on the Military jet flying to Japan Dr. Wilson receives another call from Dr. Hamaski She tells him that they have moved the Mermaid body to a cold locker on the island to keep it from decomposing. Dr. Wilson relays the message to the doctors.

"My only concern is that if there are other Mermaids in the area will they attack us or other ships in the area and blame us for the death of their Mermaid." Robert said.

"I am sure they know it was tsunami that killed the Mermaid, not the Navy this time

We really need to see for ourselves then we can know what killed the Mermaid." Dr. Wilson tells them.

After landing in Oahu, refueling they were in the air to Japan. After landing at the airbase, they soon were on a Navy ship on their way to the Island Aogashima in the Pacific to meet with Dr. Hamaski and her staff. On the way to the Island while eating in the ships galley Robert ask Dr. Wilson a question.

"Once we are on the Island and viewing the Mermaid who will be proving security for us to and from our ship. As you know doctor it is very deep waters around the island and how are we going to know if we are about to be attacked by the Mermen when we are in our tender traveling to and from our ship and…" Robert is interrupted.

"Robert, the Mermen tails glow in the water just like the Mermaids, that's how they know who the other Mermaids are. It will tell them we are coming. Plus we have our own security with us as always. Dr. Wilson concludes.

As the Navy ship stops north of the island Dr.Wilson, Brandy, Jing and Robert with security board the ships tender. They were lowered to the ocean watching the large swells heading towards the island. As they head towards the island Robert looks over the side of the tender and he see's several glowing lights in the water traveling towards the tender. One of Roberts arms is hanging over the side of the tender when a wet human webbed hand grabs his. Roberts notion is to pull the hand up towards the tender which also keeps him from falling into the water. As Robert pulls the hand and arm up the side of the tender a Merman appears smiling. He stars into Roberts eyes and tells him "We want the body of the mother of our children. Bring her to me soon. We will be waiting." The Merman slides into the water. Robert turns to Brandy and Jing also looking at Dr. Wilson and tells them what just happened. They sit looking at each other and smile.

"I knew something like this would happen." Brandy tells them.

"Ok, let's tell Dr. Hamasaki and see if they will work with us to return the body to the Mermen, I can tell you we will and the Navy will have problems with all the Mermaids if we don't return her today. Let's take all the pictures and small samples and share them with the Japanese. I think they will buy into our approach.

"I think you are right doctor." Brandy replies.

"I think they might but will want something more, knowing the Japanese." Robert smiles and concludes.

After several hours of negations and promising special equipment for their ship and the deal is completed.

In the Pacific ocean three miles off the coast of the island of Aogashima, part of the Japanese Islands, the NOAA ship sits quite in the water awaiting for the Mermen to arrive. Brandy, Jing and Robert with Dr. Wilson look over the starward side looking for the Mermen to retrieve the body of the Mermaid. Also standing on the deck were deck hands awaiting the orders of Dr. Wilson to retrieve the Mermaid body from the ships refrigerator. This was a somber time on the ship as the very person they promised to protect was now dead. Brandy, Jing, Robert and Dr. Wilson have discussed this with each other but now just had an uneasy feeling about the Mermaids and in a few minutes there gut feeling also sometimes referred to as Actum Razor would play itself out on the deck of the ship. As Dr. Wilson looks through his vernaculars at the ocean a dark figure about two hundred yards off the star ward side of the ship appears. Dr. Wilson calls out to Brandy, Jing and Robert.

"Out two hundred yards, what is that dark…." Dr. Wilson is interrupted by Brandy.

"I think it is a school of dolphins, wait there are Mermen hanging onto their fins, they have weapons, spears with them, there are hundreds of them and they are coming fast. Wait, look Robert, Dr. Wilson, from the Bow there is another pod it is the Mermaids they are ridding Killer whales towards the dolphins. They also have weapons.

Wait they are attacking the Mermen. O my gosh, they are protecting us against the Mermen attack.

As Brandy, Jing and Robert with Dr. Wilson along with the deckhands watch the battle between the two Merman Pods. The entire crew watch in horror. Some of the Mermaids stand on the Killer Whales as they swam through the pod of Dolphins, Mermen are crushed and thrown into the air and others swam off into the blue. One could see the direction they swam off to as the light from there fins light up as they swam off into the deep. One killer whale came towards the ship as all the doctors stood in amassment watching every move. To the shock of everyone ridding on the killer whale hanging onto the large fin is the old Mermaid waving with her web hands as if she is in a victory parade or the victor of the battle that just took place. Brandy goes down the gang plank to meet the old Mermaid. She looks at Brandy as she sits on the killer whale and tells her telepathy.

"The Mermen were renegades and that is the end of them. As you can see Mermaids rule and we understand you are trying to protect us. We love you Brandy, Jing and

Robert I will see you soon. The killer whale dives into the water with the old Mermaid hanging onto the Hugh fin.

As Brandy, Jing and Robert return home on the north shore on Oahu, Robert is sitting on the lany thumbing through reports he received from other researchers who reported seeing human like people, half fish and half human in Californias oldest lake two and half hours north east of San Francisco and two and half hours north west of Sacramento.

Robert looks up from the report over looking his glasses and ask.

"Brandy do you know this research may also bring us in contact with another tribe of Mermaids. These researchers said there is a volcano named Mt. Konocti and in the lake fishermen report many Mermaids."

Robert leans over to Brandy and ask.

"Can you get me a beer babe." He ask.

"Sure" Brandy smiles and replies.

"This research ladies." Robert stops and looks at Jing and smiles, and ask.

"Are you ladies ready for some more exciting research contacting Mermaids and Merman.in a lake in northern California." Robert ask.

"Yes Brandy replies, Jing yells yes, lets go and check it out. They reply.

"If you guys want to learn about this lake it is called Clearlake but there is nothing clear about it. It was once a very deep lake but they have let cement fill in over the years, however one of the researchers from UC Davis reports he found a cave just outside this area named Buckingham that goes under the volcano. He only went a few hundred yards and he saw what looked like a man hiding behind some debris he was scared and swam out of the cave." Robert reports.

"I have the actual report here." Jing shows her dad.

"Let me read that report." Brandy ask.

"So these researchers were sent to Clearlake to evaluate the mercury levels in the lake and just stumbled onto this possible Mermaid. Interesting." Brandy said out loud.

"So when can we all head up to this lake." Ask Brandy.

"Let's check with the boss first, then go." Robert replies.

Robert looks at both women waiting for a reply, he

nods his head as to say yes lets go but he knows from past experience with his boss to get his blessing before doing anything.

"You are right Robert lets go in and see the boss and run this past him. After all we all just went through a lot almost getting killed." Brandy said.

"You are right and I think we should spend some time on RR and surfing, laying on the beach relaxing. It just isn't healthy going from one stressful event to another and I am truly concerned about Jing having to much on her palate right now with her dissertation coming up." Robert tells Brandy.

"Good decision Robert, let's grab our boards and hit the surf, unplug the phone turn off the cell phones and for the next week we are doing nothing but relax ok you guys." Brandy tells both of them.

All three of them drive to north shore and paddle out to catch some waves. After catching a few sets they are sitting on their boards and stare at each other and start laughing. Robert looks at Brandy and smiles and said.

"Hay babe, this is great but what about the Mermaids in the lakes and...." Just then interrupted by Jing.

"Look you guys we can't just shut down when we know these Mermaids may need our help, they have been suffering from all that sonar research. As scientist we owe a duty to protect this species. But they are very creepy to look at." All laugh and nod their heads in agreement and paddle into the beach.

Later that day inside NOAA office Robert, Brandy and Jing sit at the conference table with Dr. Wilson.

"Ok we have been able to successfully stop all sonar

testing by the Navy and any private contractor until we either relocate the Mermaids and Merman and children or a new administration in DC. So we must develop some plans to protect them and still keep this secret from the public." Jing speaks up.

"Why do we have to keep this a secret from the public doctor." She ask

"Because if we let the general public know there will be individuals who will want to exploit this population just like men have for centuries starting with slaves, women and children. There are some very bad actors in our society and we must protect them at all cost, any questions." He ask.

"Now the reason I called you guys here is that I have to cancel your time off after talking with the president a few hours ago. She told me that we must develop a plan to protect this population from the public right away. So tomorrow morning I have a KC 130 on the tarmac at 0700 hours that will fly all three of you Travis Air force base in northern California. You will be met by Governor Brown, who is by the way in the lope and very supportive. He will supply you with anything you need. You will drive to Lake County doctors. Explore the caves on the mountains for Mermaids. Because the Chief of Staff at the White House told me that some fisherman got wind that these Mermaids may be living in the lake. This lake has some of the largest Bass fish in the country. Clearlake is the oldest lake in the Country, the likely hood of them living in those waters is real." "Any questions doctors."

Robert, Brandy and Jing look at Dr. Wilson and smile, Robert tells him

"We will be on the tarmac at 0700 hours tomorrow doctor if you need to talk with us before we fly out.

"Keep me informed doctors and no eating the Bass the Mermaids may need that food." Dr.Wilson tells everyone.' And everyone laughs.

"No problem doctor". Robert replies to Dr. Wilson and all three walk out of the conference room.

Inside the NOAA Toyota SUV on the way home Brandy ask Robert.

"So what do you think, did we get a good assignment or did we just get screwed again."

All three laugh out loud.

"So does anyone have any ideas how we can save the Mermaids from destruction all over the world." Robert ask the group.

I think we have already started doing that, we have stopped the Navy testing there Sonar. I think we need to locate those pods of Mermaids all over the world and just find out what there needs are and what we can do to protect all of them. Brandy replies.

Let's go home so I can wash all our clothes "Jing said."

As the family drives towards the north shore a calm feeling is felt among all of them. Living in the Hawaiian Islands provides a feeling of tranquility and a calmness enters one's body.

"Does anyone have any data on Mermaids in lakes anywhere, I just never have read anything about them living in lakes other than the Lock Nest Monster." Brandy said.

"Yes, we have data from reports of direct sittings in lakes and boats found with spears into the hulls." Robert reports.

"To answer your first question Robert all we have to do to protect Mermaids through out the world is to locate the pods of them, make contact, provide protection for them, and any other needs for them including medical, food and possible sunken ships or some type of under water shelter from sharks and fishermen and other humans. Jing concludes.

"So that's all we have to do with three of us," Robert looks at Jing and shakes his head."

"Actually, Dr. Wilson has approved a new department and funding with a staff of sixty two. Jing tells Robert. "How did you find out about this new department and the funding ask Robert. Dr. Wilson's assistant just told me in the bathroom and she said not to tell anyone. Dr. Wilson wants to surprise you guys this after noon at the staff meeting.

That after noon Dr.Wilson presented Dr. Robert, Jing and Brandy with a letter assigning all three of them to the new "OMD" Ocean Mermaid, Department" Also assigned to Dr. Walters new department is one of NOAA ships.

After the staff meeting Robert, Brandy and Jing drive home to the north shore. On the way home they all share their thoughts where they should start and how are they going to protect all of the Mermaids all over the world from all the outside influences and our own Navy and their contractors.

Now at home north shore Robert ask Brandy for a beer while he gets set up his portable desk in the Liany. Now all three sitting in the lanay, Jing drinking her diet Pepsi and mom and dad drinking their Budweiser light. A light wind blows off the ocean and Robert says'. No matter where we go or what we do, there is no better place on earth than the North Shore of Ohau". Brandy and Jing hold their drink in a suite with their bottle.

Robert speaks up and said "I think we need to set aside searching lakes for this population. The reason for this decision is we to address their needs in our oceans through out the world. Once we develop protocols of inaction with this population and support measures them possibly we can develop protocols for all of the populations in the oceans.

"What do you guys think about Dr. Davidson." Brandy ask. "He was nominated for some honor for his research on a possible lost tribe and…why are you asking Brandy?"

"Oh he asked me out to dinner tomorrow night." Brandy replies with a smile. "So are you going out to dinner with him.? Jing ask.